Fishermen's Tales

www. fishermenstales . com

Cheers

Peter

For Margaret and John

Fishermen's Tales

Peter Kennedy

J PUBLISHING COMPANY LTD.

London

A catalogue record for this book is available from the British Library.

ISBN 978-1-907989-07-0

ISBN 978-1-907989-07-0

00799

9 781907 989070

Printed in Great Britain

Notes on the Text

By James Marshall President of The Historians of England North

Miracle is an overused and misleading word, covering a multitude of sins, but the fact that you're holding this book in your hand, reading these words, seems, to this secularist, a conspiracy of circumstance.

Eight years ago while building a kitchen extension in the back garden of his northern home, a retired school teacher found a rusty clasp bearing a remarkable crest. A fan of TV archaeology, he called Dig the North and six days later, home improvements postponed, a Channel 4 camera crew was camped in his suburban garden.

After several days of painstaking excavation, the team eventually unearthed a corrosion damaged wooden chest with Decorated Gothic brass trimmings. Inside were candle stick holders, metal cups, a collection of parchment and human thigh bones. Several sections had been destroyed or damaged and though preliminary forensic examinations dated the manuscripts to the Plantagenet era, the orthography revealed an awareness of the 1470 Chancery Standard. Indeed the sophistication of the Northumbrian scribal and dialectical form identified it as Early Modern English for many linguists.

For three years, two Cambridge professors laboured to translate the text, attuning it to the contemporary ear, then, just as the manuscript was being prepared for publishers, the plot thickened. While watching a repeat of the Channel 4 show, a town clergyman remembered his departing predecessor showing him a casket containing similar looking parchments. Excitedly he rushed into the vestry and exhumed four chapters written in the same elaborate calligraphy.

Though deemed to date from the Jacobean era they were undoubtedly from the same series of stories and seemed to explain certain inconsistencies in the original tale. Whereupon, the church, which had been in desperate need of restorative funds, suddenly received a charitable windfall and local press reports sparked a series of similar 'discoveries'. Thus began a Cinderella style search in the historian world as experts tested documents for authenticity and rejected an annoying array of forgeries.

Three months after announcing they'd given up chasing red herrings, a glass slipper was found. A pensioner in a Galloway village found a document in an attic box that had been passed down through his family for generations. Among the sepia-tint portraits, certificates of birth and death and his great grandmother's love letters was a short piece that the team unanimously agreed was a conclusive chapter.

The first edition, of what became known as Fishermen's Tales, was in the shops selling steadily, largely in academic circles, when the saga took a final twist. A Yorkshire historian working in the archive department of a local museum (yours truly) contacted the publishers regarding an intriguing discovery. Given Fishermen's Tales for Christmas he noticed geographical correlations to a document that the museum had been displaying in the People's Collections since the war.

Though everyone involved in the project agreed with the assessment, there was division in the ranks regarding authenticity. The diary dated from the Georgian era (before the unifying influences of Johnson) and though no dates were mentioned it appeared to have been used to record a story from a much earlier era, a story that (though second hand) mentioned characters from the original texts. The translators Heyne and Socin quarreled about the tale's inclusion, with the latter threatening to quit the project unless the publishers desisted with the doubtful chapter. This revised edition, complete with epilogue, now offers the reader what is widely regarded as the definitive Fishermen's Tales at the time of press.

The final word then must go to the man instrumental in helping realise this fabulist collection, Professor Charles Heyne: "True, the historical accuracy of this final chapter or epilogue cannot be conclusively verified, but we are convinced it is an authentic reproduction of an original parchment long since lost.

"Though it's a comparative neophyte, it's literary tenor and linguistic tics bear all the hallmarks of its venerable forbears. Moreover, it clearly references and reflects previous tales, providing the sense of completion that we felt secured its imprimatur."

That said, considering the unorthodox gestation of this incredible text and its continual mutation, we at THEN will endeavour to maintain an open mind regarding source material. The society will remain a proud conduit for this literary receptacle – who knows, maybe there are plenty more Fishermen's Tales in the sea.

'The fishermen hung the monkey o so many years ago'

Behind the Net Curtain

Once upon a town, a darkness fell.

It rolled over the moors like a freezing fog, appeared on the hilltops like enemy hordes, crept down into the valleys like hungry wolves and wreaked through the land like the reaper's scythe.

Black death. A curse, a blight, an absence of light, spread itself through the streets, tumbriled door to door touching shoulders, chest and head, claiming its tithe and draping a pall of loss and grief in its wake.

Soon, amidst the stacked bonfires of bloated animal corpses the faces of men, women, children appeared as the pestilence outstripped the survivors' hurried burial rites. Funeral pyres coughed out spumes of smoke and a bilious phlegm of soot settled on the roofs, etched into the building cracks, the lines of faces and hearts of men. But the dreaded fires served a practical purpose, visible for miles they became beacons in the night, sending unwitting warnings along the coast to neighbouring towns.

They saw it first of course, being a headland. Jed Carty, gathering crab pots down by the harbour, had chilled at the startle of red from Scarsdale, or maybe Bridley Pike, 20-25 miles south, that meant they must prepare. Replacing his bait and bricks, he rowed to shore, moored his coble and ran up the sands to tell his tale.

They'd known it was coming but had lowered their heads and doubled their workload. For weeks tinkers' rumours had been moving up country of a terrible disease that had stricken the South. Inter-town trade had dropped off to necessities, until only the brave, the desperate or greedy would risk hauling their wares to the next village. When the messages stopped they waited, stultified by a mix of hope and denial.

Something made Maggie look up from her stitching ('jus like doin' 'is vests 'cept bigger'). The bairns were alright, Annie was playing in the dirt with Mary Roberson's daughter and Joe chasing a dog across the cobblestoned Kop, each bare foot slap an unwelcome reminder of shoes. She looked around and saw Jack at the top of the ladder struggling to drape a mass of nets over The Bridge without spilling his beer.

He smiled and she waved. It felt like Carnival Day, for the first time in weeks they'd managed to shake off the fear and enjoy themselves. The free beer helped.

"Backward and inbred? That'll show 'em" said Seth, wiping sweat from his brow and whistling through his broken tooth where his father hit him with a poker as a boy.

"Aye" said Davy, handing him a beer, "and when they come a knockin' we'll not let 'em in."

"Aye" said Seth "when the' come crawlin', on their knees, beggin' for 'elp, black and stinkin' with pox, puss weepin' from their sores, cryin' out in God's name for mercy, we'll not let em in…it'll be so sweet."

"Aye" said Davy, eyeing Seth warily, "sweet".

Two days earlier the Crofters had gathered in the village square by the war memorial to decide what must be done.

"We have our own wells, our own livestock, grain and fruit supplies" he stopped, peered dreamily at an undefined point in the distance, turned slowly and raised his hands "and we're surrounded by food!" A roar went up, half laugh, half cheer. Bull Henderson! Father John had called the committee meeting for dusk, but as he arrived Henderson was already amidst a little preliminary rabble-rousing with the fishermen and their wives, so many of whom had inexplicably turned out early.

"The sea! She's never let us down. Let her be our provider and our protector. This is our home, our castle" he gestured towards the Town Wall, "and we have the greatest moat in the land. The cliffs protect us to the East, all we need do is fortify The Bridge and we're an island."

He paused and changed tack, allowing them time to absorb before lowering his tone to intimate and conclusive. He came down from the podium and stood amongst the crowd.

"We sit tight. Self-contained. Self-sufficient. Just like it used to be. Our forefathers survived without them and now, if we want to survive, we must prove we can too."

They drew straws and Jackie Stubbs took the stand next. Sensing the mood of the crowd the fat faced publican made a 'diplomatic decision' to follow the balance of power.

"It's our only logical option" he blustered, jowls wobbling, spittle flying, as he tried to whip up some credible indignation. "Few have ventured beyond The Bridge in the past weeks...and now, since the fires were seen..."

It's good for trade he told himself, preferring to believe he was hard-nosed and self-serving rather than cowardly and servile. At 48 his days were occupied by his business, his wife and his refusal to admit that the civic power he'd inheriting from his father along with The Ship Tavern had been squandered in pursuit of easy living and profiteering. He caught Bull's eye and was thrown by confusion as the big man tossed him a conspiratorial wink.

"It's too late now. We must think of ourselves, our families, our livelihoods..." What was Bull's game? "They're on their own."

Thinking about *his* speech, Father John missed Stubbs' capitulation. He cast his eyes to heaven and waited for direction. It was a constant source of annoyance to him that no matter how many books he read, how many words and ideas he stored, how often he performed, he would never match Henderson as an orator. He found it difficult enough on the Sabbath, with a captive audience, but now Bull had pre-empted him, undermining all his ecumenical pleas with an appealing common sense.

They were on a headland, as were Scarsdale, so the towns that lay inland were unlikely to have seen the warning fires. What would become of their sister town, three miles to the west? We must go and warn them Father John had disclaimed but his ardour cooled when it was made clear that he, as an infection risk, wouldn't be readmitted. Mercifully their village had yet to be touched by death and that's how they aimed to keep it. Okay, he conceded, but what of the healthy, seeking sanctuary from the sick - should they turn them away in their hour of need, should they spurn their fellow man, or should they extend the hand of brotherhood? Here he'd managed to open debate.

That afternoon as he'd mindlessly administered blessings (it seemed the whole village wanted to be rebaptised) he'd mentally cast through the Bible searching for the passage that would touch the Christian in his kinfolk - 'The eternal god is thy refuge' Deuteronomy 33:27; 'If thine enemy be hungry, give him bread to eat; and if he be thirsty, give him water to drink' Proverbs 25:21; 'thou shalt not bear any grudge against the children of thy people, but love thy neighbour as thyself' Leviticus 19:18; - but now as the brute north wind reddened his cheeks, and he contemplated the fire and brimstone ahead, it all sounded like empty rhetoric.

He felt impotent and estranged. Since the fires, rumours had spread that Bull wanted to brick-up The Bridge and guard the ramparts with muskets and canons. Entering the village, where the road bottlenecked to a land strip hemmed on one side by the cliffs and the other by the docks, was an arch, heralding the welcome known as The Bridge, though no one could remember seeing it used in accordance with its name. Protect that 300 yard stretch and the headland was impregnable by cankerous foe. And, though nothing had been announced, nor Bull's name mentioned, confessional box whispers provided Father John with the clues he needed to know Henderson had been out tub-thumping. Support was spreading through the community, he could feel it - invidious self-interest.

At last week's congregation, Pat Manus had taken him, quite roughly, by the elbow and stepped into the shadows: "When's the church gonna take action father? People can't live in this limbo forever. We need guidance." Pat was a good Christian, but a frightened Christian. Like many others his nature had been discoloured by paranoia.

On Tuesday, as he pruned The Rectory ivy, Tommy McAnn, taciturn, stoical, principled, had approached and uttered a couple of cryptic lines before walking off in an irritatingly purposeful manner leaving Father John wondering if the visit was especially, or in passing?

They wanted to brick The Bridge and save themselves, it was natural, but they wanted to do it with a clear conscience. Bull, for all his irrepressible passion, couldn't provide that.

What was it Tommy had said...? He worked to recall the unusual phrasing: "It's time we put an end to all this talk Father." No, that was his opening line, it was the second that was puzzling, ambiguous, something about The Bridge...

He had it, but from a different angle, like he was suddenly standing on the other side - "my great great grandfather laid that foundation stone" - and he knew, before he'd formulated the phrase, that he'd found the means to win over the townsfolk - Psalms 24:7: 'Lift up your heads. O ye gates; and be ye lift up, ye everlasting doors; and the King of Glory shall come in. Who is this King of Glory? The LORD strong and mighty.'

Galvanised he took the floor and delivered a crafty ecclesiastical sermon - 'close the everlasting doors on our neighbours and we also shut out God' - with an architectural subtext that played on their instinctive resistance to change. He knew many would be fearful of permanent damage or alteration to their beloved Bridge. History was vague about its heritage, placing it sometime between the dark ages and the border wars, but debate still raged over whose ancestors had transported the limestones up from the Grimley quarry.

He pitched them a scenario in which they could save The Bridge and salve their souls and as that understanding spread through the crowd Bull's militant stance was gradually forgotten. The remainder of the meeting descended into a theological debate on which materials would or would not impede the Lord's influence. Bull continued to petition hard for 'wooden gates at least', but the mood had swung towards compromise and Father John maintained a dignified silence. If allegiances were being drawn, then no one wanted Him to desert them, not when death was in the air.

When Bull was satisfied he'd exhausted all his avenues (Father John watched fascinated as he worked the angles like a rat in a warren) he deftly executed a volte-face in a long slow arc which eventually aligned him with his adversary. By the meetings close he convinced many they'd long been partners.

Each fisherman was to donate two nets, a team would drag them up from the boats while the wives set about stitching them together with needle and twine. A second team would climb ladders and drape the nets - stitched rigid, doubled, tripled, chainmailed - over the archway until they hung like a semi-permeable mesh that, theoretically at least, kept plague out but welcomed piety in.

Bull's support became so voluble that by the time he promised 'free beer and bread for all volunteers' Father John had to stifle a smile and remind himself that since the defeat of his proposed mercy mission, any 'victory' for him was essentially pyrrhic.

"It's settled then" Bull stood arms aloft in the centre of the square determined to take advantage of the rising spirits. "Tomorrow we start with the nets, but tonight we celebrate. Everyone up to The Ship for a drink!"

A drink! A drink! Jackie Stubbs cursed. All his speeches ended with a drink, and whenever Bull promised drinks, *he* ended up out of pocket. The first round, on Henderson, would go straight to his slate (which hadn't been paid for months), followed by several more for friends and business associates into the early morning. The next few hours would be spend in a fit of agitation as he bathed in the residue of Bull's kudos while counting the pennies, wondering how much longer he could afford to fund his associate's empire building.

That was five days ago. Celebration had dissolved, shadows deepened and the seagulls stopped following the trawlers into the docks.

Shipwrecked

They're pulling up the wreck from the seabed again. Twelve middle-aged men with twelve drunken schemes.

Enduring early retirement, propping up the bar, staving off the inevitable with drinking and bickering. Occasionally, when their alcoholic intake coincides, they've even been known to agree. Listen. Can you see the sediment rising?

"I 'eard it was struck by lightnin'"

"Aye, as they set off a cabin boy looked back te port wannit?"

"Naw, it was whistlin'. One of the men was whistlin' in the wheel'ouse and they got caught in a storm."

"Whistlin'? Isn't that supposed te be good luck?"

"I 'eard that one of the crew cut his toenails and Neptune got jealous 'cos 'e thought they wer offerin's to Proserpina."

"What the fuck are you on about?"

"Ye alwas ave te take it too far!"

Overhearing the conversational turn Alan and Don left off their game of pitch penny and made their way to the bar. Gradually Fish, Mally and Mick were also drawn towards the siren song. It used to be an annual event in The Pot House – wreck raising – and you might think it would abate as they got older, but it had become almost bimonthly.

"I 'eard she sailed on a Friday".

"A Frida'? What's wrong with that?" asked young Jimmy.

"Never sail on a Frida lad — that's the day Jesus was crucified."

Arthur put his beer down on the bar and, with a glint in his eye and a portentous tone, took up an anecdote.

"I 'eard the King got so sick a the superstitious sailors 'e decided to prove it was all bullshit - so *they laid the keel of a new ship on Frida', selected 'er crew on a Frida', launched 'er on a Frida' and named her HMS Frida'. They put 'er in the command of Captain James Frida' and then sent 'er out on a Frida'.*

"It was a good idea, 'cept f' one thing...neither ship nor crew were ever 'eard from again. An that's where the curse comes from..."

Sometimes in the summer when it wasn't raining they would take their beer down to the Town Wall, where, if they stood over to the right, they could see the broken tip of the bowsprit, and, at low tide, a few cracked ribs of the hull.

"Because that bit that bends round there is a beak'ead, like they 'ad on the Mayflower."

"The Mayflower? The Mayflower did not have a beak'ead!"

"Er, excuse me, but who 'ere has sailed in a tall ship? C'mon! An Rob don't even say it, because you are full o shit and ye know it!"

"What! Ar ye talkin' about The Elysium? You carn call that a tall ship? Man I've 'ad taller 'ard-ons!"

"Aye Mick, yer missus sailed taller ships than that while ye were away, ye know whara mean?"

The roles and routines shifted as they took turns at playing pro and antagonist. 'Boring' was verboten, but 'bullshitting' would lose you the floor just as quick.

"They say it's like an iceberg, y'know, three quarters underneath?"

"How the fuck would you know Mick?"

"Ye can shut the fuck up now Doc before ye start, 'cos I've sailed further

north than any a ye! I was with Mickey Finn, Clipper and Auld Edward one summer when we sailed up to the ice lands and we saw some fuckin 'uge icebergs
on that trip I'll tell ye!"

"...an 'ow would you know 'ow much was under water Mick?"

"No 'e's right Doc, they reckon there's treasure down there somewhere!"

Hundreds of fisherman sailed past it each week but three things combined
to leave the wreck untouched: One: it was situated on the edge of Hovven's Pike
– a dangerous ridge of rocks where the beach turned into cliffs - beyond the
protection of the breakwater - which created a interlocking of strong currents.
Two: less people than pretended really believed in the sunken treasure legend
(a cargo ship bound for Scotland, ran the most reliable rumour). Three: more
people than pretended believed the wreck was cursed.

"We'd need levers, winch, ropes and a small windlass..."

They ceded to Suther because, aside from his extensive fishing experience,
he'd also been head foreman when they build The Charter Mill. He was immune
to prosecution during this speech, because to question his technical knowhow
would have ruined the foundations of their fantasy. There was a lot resting on
him, but he knew his part and didn't let them down.

"Two cobles. Six man team in each, alternatin' their work..."

"Ah, will you lot give over with all that shipwreck shit." Freddie Carter, this
time, voicing the feelings of the bar's long-suffering listeners. "All this heroic talk
an in the two years I've been drinking in 'ere ar've never seen any of ye as much
as plodgin'."

But for all their squabbling the ex-fishermen had a code, a mutual respect
and support and they were quick to close ranks if a land-lubber doubted they
had the derring-do to buckle their swashes.

"Well" Don said sheepishly, "it's the curse innit. I knew three fishermen
from outta town who laughed at the curse and took a coble out one night...
they were found on the Fish Sands the next morning."

"You knew them did ye Don, personally? Or did ye 'ear from ye grandda, or your uncle or e's dog, or…"

"…Or a ghost whispered it to ye as ye passed the graveyard one night" chipped in Doc to much laughter at the bar.

"Don't mock the curse Carter. It might sound farfetched but ther's a lorra things in this world thar're beyond us, an just because ye carn understand em don't mean there isn' some truth in em."

"They say you can hear a ship's bell ringin' at night."

"Oh they do do they? Well arl tell ye what ar think, ar think you lot are fulla shit! Ye haven't got the balls to see a project like that through and ye use this curse as an excuse so ye never 'ave to foller up on ye bullshit!"

Several of the gang shuffled, eyed each other and adjusted their clothing as if readying to retaliate but when Suther returned from the toilet, still tying up his pants, all heads turned his way. If they had a leader it was him and he struggled to maintain his composure under their weight of expectation. He slowly unrolled his sleeves: "Ye sound like an expert Fred?" and as he casually picked up his beer he said in a measured tone: "So 'ow many dead sailors d'you know then?" His words resonated and in the moment's silence they pondered its benthic subtext.

Fred Carter had never been a fisherman because if he had he would have known that the twelve all had their reasons for avoiding the sea. Most of them hadn't sailed in over five years, some ten. Unlike their grandfathers and their fathers they'd never been to war, but they'd buried so many friends at sea they were trapped in a vortex of wakes. Overboard, overboard, scurvy and madness, hyperthermia, sea boils and crushed. When the roll call of ex-colleagues read like an autopsy it was easier to understand why the survivors were landlocked by fear and guilt. And for those who've run aground, another round, another round was what the seamen ordered and the publican passed out.

"So 'ow would we share the treasure?" boomed Mally, keen to restore the bonhomie.

"Split it equally."

"What twelve ways?"

"No, we'd give some to Marley's widow..."

"...an some to Annie..."

"Oh aye, of course Annie..."

"...an Florrie an the bairns as well,"

"Aye, Walter would be proud..."

As always they pledged to meet at The Quay, dawn the next day, and Matty Lee stepped forward pouring red wine on the floorboards: 'An offerin', for the long voyage. Away boys, sing...and raise the dead!' Pressed, Suther came up with a few apt lines from an old sea shanty.

'O let's raise another toast

To the Gods who watch the coast

An' please Holy Ghost don't blame us

Or let The Devil come to claim us.'

On summer days when it wasn't raining they'd take their drinks down to the Town Wall where if they stood to the right they could make it out. It wasn't always visible at first, but if they looked hard enough there it was. Sometimes looking forwards, sometimes looking back, but there's always a point, there's always a point in the distance.

The Powder Monkey

He stood on the pier at dawn, closed his eyes, filled his lungs with salt air and his head with dreams. Since a small boy he'd heard tales of great fishermen who'd travelled the world in search of adventure - his uncle Jack had sailed into Brixham where 300 boats were docked; his grandda had sheltered in the Icelandic fjords as storms battered his beam trawler, and the seamen of Brevishead steered north in search of Arcadia and off the edge of the world.

His Da had got him a start with Albert Kemp and Black Tony. His brother had traded a goose for a pair of Seth Keane's waders and his ma had knit him a fisherman's jumper with the family cable pattern and a neck so tight it made his ears bleed.

He shuffled on deck with his head lowered and mumbled greetings to the two men, too shy to meet their eyes for more than a second. In his peripheries gulls circled beyond the crab pots…and too late he noticed Blackie was holding out a hand with comical patience. He felt foolish and flushed - another social etiquette he'd been unable to anticipate. He leaned forward to fulfill it and Blackie dragged him into a headlock. "There's no need to be shy son, you're a sea dog now."

A big, bearded man with devilish eyes, Blackie held him around the neck with one powerful arm and tousled his hair. Years of sweat and fish grime had engrained itself in Blackie's leathery skin creating the swarthy hue that earned him his nickname and a sickening smell. His hands were hard and calloused from feeding ropes and scarred from fish gutting. Though he'd sit on the beach rubbing them with a flatstone, Billy's hands remained soft and girlish.

He struggled to get free. "Oh, he's a lively one" said Blackie "like a little monkey". Billy understood his role in the routine, intensifying his writhing with a grin of defiance. Blackie bend down and scratched Billy's face against his two day stubble. Billy vowed to grow himself a beard, just as soon as he'd managed some pubic hair.

"Stop messin about. We've got to get these sails up if we're to catch the tides". Albert, all jowls and big doleful eyes, was from a different generation, one too practical and world weary for roughhousing. He'd served his time under Billy's grandda and it was understood in the village that he'd accommodate the Cope family if they heard the sea calling.

Billy had landed on his feet, because The Wayfarer was the finest boat in the harbour by a stretch. One of the new 50 ketches, Albert had traded it with a seaman in Toll Lea who, it was said, won it playing cards in Marken. It had sleeping quarters for three in the hold and a small cooking area and its sails had been made by Colliers in Middle Street, London. It carried around a tonne of bait, three tonnes of salt, and half a tonne each of food and firewood for the crew. Around six tonnes of fish could therefore be carried.

His ma didn't want him to fish - too dangerous. She'd spent the last three days suggesting alternatives - 'why not shift grain at the mill...the' need 'elp at the brewery...go down the market and tell Geordie I sent ya...' It was easy for her, to push herself forward like that, but he'd never been very sociable. That was one thing he liked about the seamen - they never said much. He'd been going out mornings with Jack in the coble since he was 11 so he knew most of the mariners from hanging around the quay. Occasionally after a good catch he was allowed to sit in The Golden Fleece with Jack, his partner Bobby Ord, sometimes Tommy Welling's crew, and listen to the patter. Or appreciate the lack of it. They could play cards for hours communicating in little more than celebratory grunts, interpretive nods and practicalities concerning the pot or the next round. His dad said Jack and Bobby spend so much time together they were like a married couple. They didn't have to talk, didn't need to impress. There were unfathomable depths in their silence – life-threatening times that sat easier unsaid.

No, the sea was his place. He would learn the ropes, join a big trawler, travel the world having adventures and when he was done he'd return to the Croft, marry Mary Hodge and settle down.

Albert turned the mainsail into the wind and they surged free of the jetty. His life was about to begin…but deep underwater a single massive current moved counter clockwise.

Time seemed to last longer out there, and by the third day he'd known them for years. Such proximity bred intimacy, hard earned on land. He stifled smiles as they praised his constitution: "You're a natural son. Ther's some men, some bloody 'ard men, who were cryin' into ther vomit from day one" said Albert.

"Aye, ye auld man threw up on the quayside before he got on board." bellowed Blackie, "sed it was the fish smell." Billy introduced a little swagger to his gait and start throwing their Christian names about with more confidence.

They trawled all day without a break and filled every box with thick, healthy cod. Albert had warned them to be ready when the chance came. No matter how long they worked he knew he mustn't utter one word of complaint or even ask 'how much longer?' They thought him a boy, but he'd show them. After six straight hours he exhaled, the tension left his shoulders and his balls sat a little lower in their sack.

Just when he thought he'd managed to avoid embarrassment Blackie offered him a cigarette. 'Go on lad, don't pretend you've never had one". The truth was he hadn't, but circumstances wouldn't allow a confession, so he took his first ever drag, coughed a lung over the side. The men laughed long and hard, but Albert was understanding: "don' worry lad - y'll learn". He felt accepted. The work was done, the spirit was high and they were going home. As they head towards the sunset he could see glorious things in the offing.

"Billy!" Albert held up the fish - "These are codlings" he said "only good for feedin pigs."

"…and we've eaten all the pigs" Blackie, covering the catch boxes in salt, cackled sardonically.

"Sorry" he shouted as he tried to squeeze past. Blackie grabbed him in a bear hug. He could feel his taut muscles, their incredible strength and as he tried to wriggle free Blackie uttered the same assessment: "Oh, he's like a little monkey isn't it". Billy made a joke of it. He skipped out of arm's reach and told Blackie to fuck off, flexing the mock bravado he seemed to have earned. It felt good, it felt like, an initiation.

The angry sea slapped them across the broadside and a 30 foot swell engulfed the deck. He felt sure that this time, when the boat emerged from the foam his crewmates would be gone and 50 miles of angry water would separate him from his parents. It sounded like one of his grandda's stories, 'cept out here there were no stories, everything was too real.

It had been dark when Albert woke him with urgent eyes and dragged him onto deck where Blackie wrestled with the main sail. The storm was in its early throes, and as waves spat across the bow he caught only snatches of Albert's breathless explanation amidst the rising tumult.

"Currents....wind...same direction for miles...' he gesticulated '...when the sea shallows...nowhere for the water to go but up!"

The skipper sat him at the aft, tied a rope around his waist and knotted it to the mizzen mast. If Billy leant back he could control it with his weight, but the only thing stopping the mizzen from spinning 360 and him from being swept overboard was this symbiotic relationship with this makeshift umbilical.

Why was he here? He could have been at home, worming with Jed, walking with Mary or just sat in the Croft watching his ma stitch. Who did he think he was? Who was he trying to impress? He wasn't fearless, he wasn't a hero - he was fifteen and frightened. He didn't want to die.

He braced himself again. He was so tired. Did he sleep as the boat bobbed between each breaker? He didn't have the strength to tell anymore. He saw a strip of dawn on the horizon and reasoned that daylight meant safety.

His neck jerked up violently. The sodden rope singed skin from his palms as it whip-lashed from his weary grasp. He reared across the boat cracking his knee against the catch boxes. He scrambled on the slippery deck, unable to get a foothold. Just as he steadied himself a wall of foam hit him in the face, disorienting and pouring into his lungs. He spluttered and coughed and, as he leapt to his feet, was struck across the back of the head by the wayward mast.

When he came round Albert and Blackie's massive heads were looming over his bed. "It's over son. We made it." Albert handed him a cup of tea. "'Ere, drink summit hot lad, ye'll feel betta. Just a bang on the ead."

The storm, the mizzen, the accident, came back to him and he raised his hand to a pain he now noticed above his right eye. Bandages covered a huge bump, and their dampness, he suspected, was soaked up blood.

"An' ger a drop of this down ye an arl. Ar think you've earned it." Blackie tipped a little whisky into his mug before taking a swig himself. "Cheers boys."

The congratulatory mood continued - they were going home and with a hull full of cod. "There'd be a few quid in it for ye" Blackie said, "an y'll have to beat the lasses off with a stick when word gets around. An arl make sure it does" he laughed.

Billy laughed too. He'd survived his first fishing trip. He was one of the men. He would have jumped out of bed right then and helped sail her home, but Albert said the weather had changed and they were waiting on the wind. So they sat on the bunks drinking and smoking while Albert whittled wood and told stories.

"Me and Joe Barnsfield once rowed for two days when the weather was lazy. That was when I had the 12 ton little dogger, so there was no cabin and very little space to store salt. We had to make it home before the catch rotted. We set off from Staleybridge on the Thursday..."

Albert's resonant voice had a soporific effect and after his third mug of whisky Billy drifted into a deep sleep. When he awoke he needed a piss badly. He propped himself up, head throbbing, guts churning. He spun as he stood up, reeled, and caught himself against the bunk just before he went down. As he made his way up the steps he passed Blackie whose shirt was open almost to the waist, a red V seared onto his chest from the cold. He lay all his weight onto Billy and slurred: "Lil' monkey. Jus like a lil' monkey". Billy wriggled free and with as much defiance as he could muster, shouted "Fuck off will ye!", because he could feel Blackie's manhood hard up against his back. He pissed quickly, vomited over the side, fell into the bunk and slept like a seabed.

When he awoke he was ruined. He would never be the same again.

Empty, hollow, sick. He vomited everything - internal organs - liver, kidneys, spleen, heart - over the side. He felt like a fish - gutted.

But he was a man. One of the lads. Why didn't he struggle, why didn't he fight? He was so drunk he couldn't defend himself!

It didn't hurt so much, it just felt wrong. Something that shouldn't be happening was happening. Something that shouldn't be there was there, making him sick in his stomach and his head. He could vomit all day, but he'd never disgorge the shame? He must never tell anyone, that was his first decision. He was a man - not a boy! not a monkey! - with that masculine capacity for silence…like Albert.

Through the twisted nightmare he'd seen a lifeline - Albert's lugubrious face in the crack of the door. Was it real? Yes! His heart leapt, he was saved, but Albert's tired jowls looked rueful, resigned - there's nothing I can do it said, this is a force beyond my control it said - and he just pulled the door shut and locked it.

The boat bobbed, the wind reasserted, but he couldn't go home. He was confused. Disgusted and confused. He'd thought about it — sex - been so far with Mary, but they weren't ready yet, he was too shy to ask. Blackie hadn't asked, just pressed himself and with that stinking breath moaned in his ear - 'you're so good, you're so good'. All that power, all that brutal lust…and him.

And now, as he touched himself he thought of Blackie - hard and strong… and vulnerable, tender even, once he'd released that hot muck on his back and lay on the bunk, falling into a stupor, stroking his hair.

Requiem for the Undead

Adam begat Joseph, Joseph begat Samuel, Samuel begat Ambrose, Ambrose begat John, John begat James, James begat William and late one Friday night William and his friends gathered in St Mary's graveyard determined to subvert the tradition.

"You 'ear 'er sobbin' first, feel a chill down yer back and a sadness in yer soul. Strange shadows stretch out across the moors and the air goes cold. Then ye see summit that wasn there before – a frail figure in a grey robe shufflin' outer the churchyard and down towards the sea. Always the same route, along the Town Wall, past the Banjo Pier an around the Bluffs path bringin' 'er back 'ere. Destined to tread the same eternal circle, forever searchin' for 'er daughter who was washed out te sea."

Beneath a willow tree, besides an unmarked grave, six boys sat cross legged in the torch-light testing each other's nerve. Teenagers, pass the bottle, trading tales - trying to scare up some fear, some incident, some feeling, because their *deepest* fear was that their lives lacked drama. In their desperation to manufacture a rite of passage they'd vowed to shed a little light on an ancient mystery, but each was hoping to cultivate a little darkness too.

They took turns – a wooden-toothed orphan baby thrown down a well, the bones of a child murderer buried beneath a farm, overzealous gravediggers who unearthed the screams of hell – before an authentic note was struck and Will became the one believed.

"She asked to be buried facin' the sea," he lent in, his voice a hefty whisper, "and, if, at midnight, ye circle 'er grave against the sundial, spit and say Grey Lady - she'll appear and take up 'er forlorn search agen."

The game was as old as time, but new to them. The Grey Lady had been passed down like an heirloom and around like a whore. Handled over and over and over ("I swear she wer' White when ar wer a lad" his da had said). Despite her reputation no one really knew her. Even the weather beaten elders shrugged nonplussed when quizzed about her roots.

Twin Doric columns and angelic wings attracted the eye and the gossipmongers – which former Crofter had afforded such elaborate engravings for their resting place? The partial erosion of the sandstone inscription added an elliptic spice to the speculation. 'Bel ved mo her of...' – the unreadable remnants were enough to fuel the legend of a woman who's 'brain snapped' when misfortune befell her family. Beyond that agreement laid a contention of half remembered rumours that had outlived their tellers.

"Ars 'eard she was a witch" Cussy had watched him throughout with his head at an unnatural angle but Will had refused to acknowledge the challenge. "Soes. Why didn ye say she was a witch?"

Many a winter's night had been warmed when Will and his family gathered round the fireplace for story time. He'd heard The Grey Lady first from his grandma (he'd been *told* he'd been told) and then his mum, and knew it word for word. He'd recounted it faithfully – no mention of black magic. His da didn't believe in witches - 'bullshit! They run us on fear' - and neither did he. It was important to get the details right, the tension, the rhythm, the pace, but when he finally turned he saw Cussy's wild eyes weren't looking to discuss storytelling.

"My da sez theys lift the dunkin' chair an ask 'er say the Lord's Prayer an she stumble so theys drown 'er."

They'd been rapt in Will's telling but piqued by this promise of witch trials. His audience shifted, but peer pressure alone didn't sully Will's tale, something unexpected had happened as he told his ghost story – he'd scared himself. Perched forward, clutching his knee double-handed, phrases, pauses, tone of voice - he was too much like his mum, and for reasons he daren't fully explore he needed to distance himself. He cast around for crowd-pleasing sensation, and from who-knows-where, he plucked one.

"Of course her hands and feet are covered in sores and as she walks she

32

leaves a trail of blood behind…like a snail…"

They'd reenacted the ceremony, stumbling around with a uneasy blend of drunken solemnity, and…nothing, just a sense of anti-climax they were now keen to assuage –

"Did anyone 'ear whisperin'?"

"Ar felt like someone was watchin' me."

"The air was cracklin', but ther' was no lightnin.'"

"Did ye notice the strong smell a jasmine?" said Will.

"Strong smell of bullshit more like!"

Cussy stepped out of the shadows, clenched. Smallpox took his eyelashes, the sea took his da, but only one returned to strip his ma of her assets and him of his self esteem. He'd taken no part, just sat beneath a tree steaming, watching, whipping himself into a spiral of self-recrimination over his subservient role. They were full of shit, but right about one thing – there was some restive spirit, some devilish mischief afoot that embittered and emboldened him tonight. He'd spent years eclipsed by Will's good looks and easy charm but never had the strength to oppose him.

"Why don' we stop fuckin about, ger a shovel and dig 'er up? That" - he mocked Will's phrasing – 'should *rouse 'er from sleep.*'"

His authority challenged, everything about Will hardened. Cussy was always looking for trouble, well if he wanted it tonight, he could have it. He was in no mood to kowtow.

"We are *not* diggin' 'er up, that's just…*wrong*."

"Aw and wor about all your circlin' an spitten' shit?"

"That's different…that was…just fun."

"Well arm *sick* of this kid's stuff!"

"But, ye carn dig up the dead, that's evil, that's a sin."

Cussy had nothing, he had nothing to lose. Will was rattled, the others

33

impressed and he raged on. If darkness was the new sovereignty then he, he'd decided, would be the new prince.

"Fuck sin! Ar'll dig 'er up an' ar'll make a necklace outer 'er teeth."

The denouement unfolded like a blanket to four view points as the group struggled to choose a corner. Cussy bundled over to the grave, high on bravado, Will broadened his gait and blocked his path. Cussy tried to shove past, Will pushed him to the ground. Cussy reached for a branch, a weapon? a shovel? – they'd never know, because the scene was rent by an unholy sound, a high keening exhortation like a belated appearance from the invoked wraith.

Will thought Cussy had landed on glass, Ben thought it was a black-headed gull, Morgan, a farmer's son, later compared it to 'a pig in a hessian sack' but there was a tacit agreement that Paul's cry had closed their morality play. And while the sound resonated they left their own thoughts behind to briefly consider their friend's. His cri de coeur struck a chord for the sacred and lay to rest the profane.

"Stop it" he said, refurling into his diffidence. "Both of ye…stop it", his apologetic whisper concluding the interlude.

They mumbled, bowed their heads, kicked the dirt and slowly dispersed, making their way along the Town Wall, six individuals, but by the time they'd reached the jetty they'd started coming together. Will and Cussy took the first steps towards rapprochement, mocking the hapless Vickers.

"So Ben ar 'ear, ye gor a good 'idin' off Watson agen?"

"E gorra lucky punch in."

"One, looks like 'e gorra dozen in te me!"

"Well ar was drunk."

"They reckon if ye rub beetroot and vinegar into the scars they'll go down."

"And 'orse shit – rub sum a thar in an all."

The others laughed, Paul sighed, shook his head and stared out to sea. Sheep begat sheep. Cussy was an arsehole, but he was right – fuckin' kids stuff.

Paul hadn't told anyone but he had a baby brother, Andrew, who'd died. He'd only been three at the time and couldn't remember, but his mam often monologued when she'd had a few drinks

He didn't think he was mad or anything but that night he felt, as he often did before he dropped off to sleep, the weight, the gentle pressure of his brother sitting at the foot of his bed.

Shibboleth

Don't say a word she told him.

He'd been complaining since they left the village - "Mam arm all itchy."

"Ssshhh Luke. Ar've told ye not to say that."

"But mam I am!"

She'd told him, told him repeatedly, but he was too young to understand, just like he couldn't understand that she ignored his other question - 'are we there yet?' – because she had no idea where they were going. Now, on the horizon, she could see a chance of salvation that needed his silence.

"Whar are ye gonner say when we get there Luke?"

"Can ar 'ave a carry?"

"No! What are ye gonner say when we get there?"

"Carry!"

He'd cried himself to sleep last night, *and* awake the next morning. His weeping and moaning of hunger pains gradually gave way to a sob, a whimper, then nothing. Three, she thought, was too young to understand futility. She was so tired. She felt sure she'd have collapsed by now had it not been for the bairns. He reached up – 'Mam. Carry' – and she reached down inside herself and pulled something up that she didn't know was there.

"Okay, but promise ye'll be quiet. No more about bein' itchy"

She hoist him up on her hip and turned to check Sarah. It's going to be all right she told them again. She was so tired. It was only a few hundred yards now. She could see the guns, and was scared, but the alternatives were inconceivable. She trudged along the wet sand dragging the children with the promise of hope.

After the nets party the Crofters awoke, heads heavy, to find Bull the self-appointed chief of security - "I want four men on The Bridge at all times - two at the gate, two more rest in the Engine House ready for the next shift." Many wondered if they'd missed something at the meeting, but no one questioned his actions. The fearful and confused found a place to crouch behind his purposeful attitude, abdicating responsibility while reassuring themselves someone was in charge.

Mally couldn't give a fuck about The Bridge, his first thought on hearing Bull's security proposals had been for his brother, away at sea.

"'Ere! Whar about our Terry! 'E's out fishin' with Danny Lynch. Surely we're gonner let him back in! You 'ave no right te..."

His objections were lost in an ill-tempered fugue as friends and family campaigned for absent loved ones. Mally didn't remember a conclusion. He remembered a quarantine period had been mentioned, then a drink had been mentioned and since then nothing had been mentioned. He went to the next security meeting to bend Bull's ear, talk him round, and found himself signing up as a guard. Henderson put an arm around his shoulder and took him to one side.

"Mally, I'm putting you alongside Joe by the Bluff's."

Along the North Cliffs the sea created a natural impasse, but at low tide a stretch of sand presented opportunity to those seeking refuge.

"You're a young lad but I know you're up to it – don't let me down son."

Mally was about to point out that Bull was only two years older than him until Henderson peered over each shoulder and pushed a bottle of gin under his jacket. Mally left scratching his head. He was puzzled, but what the hell, tonight he'd be pissed.

He was part of a four man team working pairs with Slater, an old friend of Bull's from his bare-knuckle boxing days. They said he'd been in jail, and didn't like to talk about it.

"Is it true" said Mally, "that you did some time in jail?"

"I don't like to talk about it" said Slater.

"Yeah, that's what I heard" said Mally, "I heard that..."

"Shut up." Said Slater raising his gun.

And that was their entire conversation since their shift started.

"A child!"

Their muskets had been pointed at the approaching figures since before they could make out the shapes.

"Some say it can be passed through the air," Bull had told them, told them repeatedly. "You don't even need to touch it. Me," he laughed, "arm not gonner wait for the whites of their eyes to see if they're bloodshot."

"I couldn't see the bairn before" Mally said. "I thought it was just a bunch of rags. An the girl an all – tucked right in behind her. Ar bet..."

"Keep your musket up" Slater said.

"Ahh, 'e's only little. He must be about the same age as our Betty's bairn."

Head bowed, leaning into the wind, the mother stopped, adjusted her bags and hitched up the infant again. She offered her hand for Sarah who pulled her shawl tighter and took it sullenly. She looked like a cod with a couple of clinging lampreys thought Mally, or limpets...or fleas.

"Stop! That's far enough" said Slater.

Difficult to tell beneath all those extra layers, but Slater thought she had that broad, big boned bucolic look that comes from tilling fields. Even from there he could see the anguish furrowed in her brow. She lowered her son to the ground in a bundle and almost slumped defeated, catching herself at the last moment.

The boy sat in the position he was put, head hanging forward like a stalk. He was looking very intently at something in the sand, or nothing.

"Please, help us. We've been walkin' for three days, haven' eaten for two. We drank the last of the water this mornin'. I'm frightened. The bairns...what do...?"

There was an awkward pause and when Joe was stumm Mally shrugged and decided he'd do the talking.

"Look luv, if it was up to me I'd let you in, but we have our orders."

"Please, show some mercy. Where should we go? We'll..."

"Ye know what's 'appenin' round 'ere, why we carn let ye in, ..."

The talkative one with the smiley face sounded like the leader, but he looked to the big mute for reassurance every time he spoke.

"Maybe if yez wer Crofters it would be different..."

"We *are* Crofters! We've been...working away."

Mally looked at Slater.

"Well Slater, whaddaya think? She *does* sound like a Crofter. D'ye know 'er?"

Mally looked at Slater for a long time, and although Slater refused to flinch, he knew Mally's eyes were wide with entreaty.

"Look!"

She pulled back the boy's coat to reveal a thick gansey. Slater recognized the same unscoured wool that his Aunt Nancy used to keep out the rain and a diamond stitch pattern that she swore brought health, wealth and happiness. It did look like a Crofter pattern, but he knew a lot of nearby towns used similar styles. Nancy sewed her initials into the bottom, but he wasn't going to get close enough to check for a regional variation.

He wanted to help her, but what about Bull, who'd told him - 'shoot first, ask forgiveness later – it's the only way to save ourselves'. He slung her a water bottle - Nancy would sit up all night knitting in the dark – and she saw a chink of light in this act of kindness.

"I'm Edith. Edith Hunt" she smiled, "you must know me 'usband George. 'E used to work on the Foyboats with..." The pause became a void even Slater felt urged to fill. "...Willy Stewart and..." She struggled, distrait with fatigue, contorted with anxiety, but before she could speak help came from an unexpected source.

"Our dad's dead" said the boy.

She sounded like a Crofter. Her accent bearing none of the flatter vowels of their sister town to the south or the salty twang of their northern neighbours but with that one innocent word, the boy had betrayed them, because Crofters didn't say 'our dad'; 'our Arthur' for their brother, 'our Annie' for their sister, but, for whatever reasons, always 'me dad', 'me mam'. Mally studied Slater out the corner of his eye.

"Please..." she said, "please..." and took an imploring step forward, more of a stumble that roused Slater's loyalties and raised his musket. He didn't like being scammed. He had a job to do. It was a sad fact, but Bull was right – they had to save themselves.

Mally made an appeal for leniency "Slater, we can't just..." but Slater's look stopped him dead.

As she picked up the boy the woman saw one more chance to evoke sympathy and nipped him hard beneath the swaddling. He never made a sound.

"Go. God be with ye" said Slater.

The woman let out a bitter laugh. He watched them trudging off, the woman encumbered by insulation, offspring and the weight of the world; her daughter sloping behind in her footsteps and something inside him didn't feel right.

"I can't help but think..." started Mally, but then checked himself "sorry Slater, ar'll..."

"No." Slater gave him a different look. "Go on."

"When ar was a bairn like, me mam used te tell me a story, from the Bible

41

a think, about a man who dreamt 'e was walkin' along the sands with the Lord. Across the sky flashed scenes from 'is life. For each scene, 'e noticed two sets a footprints in the sand; one belonged to 'im an the other te the Lord.
'E noticed that at the lowest times of 'is life there was only one set a footprints. So 'e asked the Lord, 'e sez er: "Why durin' the most troublesome times of my life, when I needed you most, did you desert me?" The Lord replied, 'My precious child, I love you and would never leave you. During your times of suffering when you see only one set of footprints, it was then that I carried you.'"

They weren't out of earshot yet. He could still help them. Slater made a deal with himself. When they turn he'd shout them back. When they turn. The bairns must turn. They're only bairns. Turn. Turn. He watched them getting smaller, smaller, though with every step it was him who was shrinking.

Curiosity Killed the Crab

Through the doorway, up the steps, along the wall and…through the doorway, up the steps, along the wall and…through the doorway…

A rabbit? A cat? A flash of white. A seagull would have flown. Between black rocks, stark, opaque, then into the cave. A rat? Must have been. A huge white rat. That's all was left. The cows were gone, were first to go, almost soundless, throats slit by thieves, butchered under darkness, meat hauled off in sacks. Farmers at dawn found stripped bovine torsos in stinking puddles of blood. Then sheep, goats, pigs, dogs; stolen, slaughtered, eaten. Only the tethered remained, under duress, and later, armed guard. Two poachers were shot dead and one crippled, clubbed across the kneecaps by Archie Bradley while trying to cut up a donkey.

He dropped the crab pots and ran along the rocks. His dad'd be gutted to see them empty again, but if he could catch that rat they'd eat meat tonight. As he crept in under the ridge he saw it again - a scumbled flash in the hueless dank, gone before he could focus. He hoist his torch to gauge the scope, and an untouched corner caught his eye. He plodged over, water around his boot rims, and traced a moss encrusted archway in the torchlight.

A hole, knee high. He kicked at the edges and felt a huge piece of tide-softened bedrock give beneath his boot. Crouching he peered through at a rough hewn rock staircase wending down into the recesses. Generations of rumours, campfire tales, about a skein of tunnels built beneath the Croft by Franciscan monks, had fallen into myth - until now.

He searched around for a rock, testing them on the walls. All he had to do was leave a chalk trail of arrows to point the way back.

He stood on the threshold of a life-changing find, determined, despite his palpitating chest and tightening throat, that this wouldn't be hijacked by his dad or his brothers - this was his.

Around corners, down passageways, echoes of dripping water swell then fade. A hum, a drone, a whorl of moans swirled through the labyrinthine chambers. It was an incredible achievement. How long had it taken them to build?

He lowered the torch. The slope was subtle, only the temperature fall indicating descent, and yet the urge to continue was a physical compulsion. Could he feel a rise and fall, an in and exhale, as the wind groaned through the stone corridors? Fear and fascination were locked in such conflict that the push and pull was tidal. He was inside a giant sea shell, or a...

There it was again! A white flash gone before he turned. Shaken he steadied himself against the wall, moisture and moss yielding beneath his fingers. He adjusted his feet for balance and then it was gone and the ground was solid again, his footing reassured. It wasn't a rat - too big, too high – so what was it?

The walls seemed to whisper. He put his ear against them, then laughed at the absurdity. What would walls say? There was someone at his back, he checked, he checked again, still not satisfied it was gravity. He'd crossed a threshold. In here anything was possible. Maybe the walls did have stories to tell. This was the Croft's history. What did the monks keep buried away? What had these walls seen? He shuddered. It was getting colder. This place held memories, secrets, this place held ghosts.

He turned, hoist the torch and looked back. Unbelievable. He'd come only 20 yards from the archway, but already in his fear chalked up three arrows.

He could turn back. He couldn't turn back. This was better than a rat, or a pot full of crabs or a cobble full of fish - this could be the town's biggest catch ever.

The wall bend off to the right, he was following a curve. Still, if he continued with the arrows that shouldn't be a problem. A sound, like iron tapped against more iron, or just an echo of dripping water? He stopped and cocked his ear. It was more like steps running, closer, closer, and then, without fading, further, then gone.

He came to a crossroads offering options left and right. His mind was sharp and he chalked a big one in a circle before he head off to the right. As he expected his options continued to multiply. Twenty yards on he faced a second choice and chalked up a two before turning left.

As he descended deeper the moisture dried, replaced with a moldering stone and an indistinct metallic smell. The darkness played tricks - he was being followed, watched, the walls censured his moves. Every 10-12 steps he had to stop and shake off the fear - it was only a cave, it was only darkness, and that sound, like a child weeping softly in the distance, was only his imagination.

He levered the stone slab with the handle of the torch. He'd reached what looked like a burial chamber. The bones of two bodies together in one tomb. A King and Queen? Between the ribs of one, a bronze chain and medal. He opened one of two smaller tombs. Little ribs, little skull, a prince? In the other was an ancient chest. He kicked at the lock, prised it with his knife. The wood was well worn, the casing rusty but solid. He straightened up to think and something caught his eye - in the clenched fingers of the threadbare corpse - a key.

Three times he reached for it, and - struggling with superstitious fears previously untapped - three times recoiled. His dad would have laughed, but in this place his reservations made perfect sense - he couldn't steal from the dead. He stood frozen, arm still outstretched, feverishly trying to justify wrong-doing. The whispering grew. Had he come all that way to return with nothing? He needed a token as proof otherwise who would believe him? That weeping again. When he called a town square gathering it wouldn't be for tales of tunnels, he needed more. The weeping, the whispering, the water expanded, filling his head but as he uncurled the key from the bony fingers they fell away to silence.

Rolls of cloth parchment, partially rotting. He untied the leather bindings and unscrolled them. In an indecipherable cursive he recognised the village name from the town hall sign and at the bottom (he knew numbers from his church learning) a date. Debate raged amongst the elders as to the age of the village. Here was a document that could unravel the riddle of their ancestry, solve the mystery of identity, maybe the long-sought proof that they outlived their sister town. They were no ordinary fishing port - they were built on an ancient burial ground; and he was no ordinary boy, he was the boy who'd unearthed the treasure.

Through the doorway, up the steps, along the wall and…through the doorway, up the steps, along the wall…It didn't make any sense. He could see the number 8 and the arrow clearly pointing to the left but when he followed them, passing 7 and 6 on the way, he re-emerged at the same place.

It was impossible. He ascended two sets of steps (he remembered them from the way in) but came out lower. He tried it again for the fifth time. He seemed to be going round in circles - two circles connected by a crossroads.

He didn't have much time, his torch was dying. He'd already burnt his scarf and his cap. Paranoia span in his head, his synapses sparking overload, fear flooding along his neural pathways, he was losing his mind.

The stone was softer here. He tried to scratch his name into the wall with his finger nail, starting the second letter before abandoning the futile legacy. This was the mark he would leave? From the town's most famous son to this! It was all over. He was crying, screaming, clawing at the wall, his nails breaking, blood ran down his hands, biting at the stone in frustration and terror. The susurration intensified - the buzzing of flies feeding on corpses, the screams of sinners sucked into the pit, eternally punished for deathly transgression, for violation of sacred tombs.

He screamed as the last of the torchlight flicked, then wept. He traced his way along the wall, waiting for his eyes to acclimatise, but there was no light to work with. They'd never let him leave, that much was clear, but edging into the darkness he tried again…

Through the doorway, up the steps, along the wall and…through the doorway, up the steps, along the wall and…

The Sky is Falling

Never tread on graves, burn egg-shells or cut your hair when the moon is waxing. Black cats, broken mirrors, horseshoes, magpies, cracks. His grandma made his mother burn salt for six days once when she caught her picking berries after Michelmas.

James was a modern man, times had changed, they knew things now, they listened to reason, all that superstitious nonsense was dying out - but still, he had to admit, he was shitting himself!

Red sky at morning, sailors take warning; but when dark clouds descended until they hung overhead almost touchably close, no one was singing nursery rhymes. It was four days before anyone looked up at the angry undersides of those storm clouds and thought to ask - 'why hasn't it rained?' No one answered, and no one asked again.

For eight days they waited for the weather to break - a gap in the clouds, a glow on the offing - and then they stopped waiting for that and started waiting for something else, something nameless that made them grateful for this darkened existence.

No birdsong broke the oppressive mood, no dog bark, no cat cry nor rat scurry. Livestock moaned and chewed at their tethers. A horse broke free and ran thrashing into the sea. It took four men twenty minutes to wrestle the crazed beast back to shore, and all their will power not to follow it.

As November days shortened, night and day merged and minds got lost in the dusk. Scores of believers assailed the church with the same fevered abandon, descending on St Hild's to plead with God and tear at Father John's cassock as he passed down the aisles. One night, awoken by tapping on the church door, he offered his lamp out into the darkness to see Peggy Casey curled up against the headstones praying, her body half frozen.

Many refused to leave their homes. Bodies, confused, closed down and escaped into luminous dreams. Others, convinced an angry God was punishing them, huddled before homemade alters crossing themselves until their heavy eyes demanded sleep.

Their ancestors had worshipped the sea, the sun, the wind as gods, only now could James understand those simple minded beliefs. Several of the older parishioners proposed a sacrifice from the end of the breakwater, but since the cod yield had dropped no one could afford to waste a goat. On the beach oaths were muttered as sacrificial burlap sacks bobbed out to sea filled with fruit, vegetables, hand crafted effigies, and once, a kitten.

Smoke billowed down the coast and firelight halos piqued their conscience sending them, heads bowed, inland. The children traded stories of screams skimmed off the ebony sea at night. 'Seagulls!' adults chided, full knowing they'd flown before the rats.

His ma had spent a lifetime of preparation, she'd been raised with an apocalyptic mindset. When she was a girl they'd had more Armageddons than weekends. His father too, while not superstitious, had been telling him since he was three that they were 'all going to hell'. And now, when it looked like the doom mongers might be right they were too busy counting backwards to enjoy their triumph.

Nancy Moran was found wandering the moors, delirious, biting her wrists and screaming at horror in the clouds. As James watched the 'daylight' thicken to the more natural lightlessness of evening he almost understood how those louring shadows could persuade her to take the tempting step towards insanity. Difficult to say since they lost the sun, but he guessed they'd almost finished their afternoon shift, and much of that time had been spent avoiding eye contact with cloud demons cackling beneath formidable frowns.

Bull had stepped up security, convinced them they needed four more men on the Moors Wall, three more men on the coast - two on the Sandwell Char and a look-out in the lighthouse - to combat his surety that they would come from the sea. He played on their paranoia…cultivating. Paranoid? Not James, he preferred to call it vigilance. It was rare that he sided with Bull, but he was a practical man who agreed they must protect against the genuine danger of infection. That's why he had volunteered for security shifts. The fishing fleets had been halved, the farms had cut labour to family and market days had become bleak, desolate affairs. The position carried no wage, but Bull promised everyone bread and vegetables for their families. As work disappeared and the streets deserted, paranoia became currency and reason a difficult commodity to find.

The clouds pressed down like an etherised cloth, or a pillow, and the life force drained from the town. It was difficult to stay awake. Tom had a small blade from his mother's kitchen that he pressed into his palm whenever James patrolled. James had been learning to read and had two pages of parchment (traded with a traveller who still owed him two more for those ales) that he unfolded whenever alone. As he pieced the syllables together his eyes flicked anxiously to the Gate wall for Tom's returning torch. He'd never had chance to test his theory, but he felt sure reading was considered bad luck.

Now, as they sat out their remaining minutes James' head nodded, and despite the 11 hours sleep he'd had the previous night, he drifted into a nether world of dreams. The mechanism had gone in his body clock.

A cry! James leapt out of his reverie and threatened his gun into the night. A wave, a ripple, moved across the hinterland, shuddered his body and he let off a round into the darkness. A huge crow, perched on rubble out in no-man's land, watched with a preternatural patience.

Tom fell backwards from his stool:

"What the 'ell ya doin!"

"There's summat out there, ar can feel it" said James, already reloading. He was confident he could ward off any forthcoming evil with a smoothbore long guns Bull had conjured up. That's what he'd chosen to believe and he'd stick with it unless forced to reconsider.

"Yeah, a crow, I eard it n'all but arm not gettin crazy."

He ignored Tom, he felt something, and with gun butt wedged firmly under his chin, traced an intent semi circle with his weapon.

"Nah, it's more, much more, an arm gonna be ready when it gets ere."

Tom jumped up and tried to prise the musket from his hands.

"Keep it together man. Ye can 'ear the shots in the village. Ye know whar it's like, it wone take much to panic 'em."

Their tussle slowed and froze - James with gun cocked, Tom with barrel tilted at a restraining angle - as they spied a glow moving along the cliffs towards the moors.

Maybe it was the change in light, their eyes had spent six days acclimatizing to a lack of colour, but the flickering luminosity immediately struck them as unnatural. In the absence of moonlight it floated, disembodied, hovering among the trees. Neither of them moved, their gaze fixed on the photism. Time slowed and stretched.

"Ignis fatuus" James said to himself.

"What?" said Tom.

Then, clearer, breath like a dray horse in the freezing torch light, James spat the plosive consonants into the night.

"Corpse candles."

He'd been drawn back to the magnetic north.

Smaller than he remembered, The Bridge was a welcome sight as he plodded down through the freezing fog. Not quite the triumphal arch of a returning emperor, but, between two torches, its silver curtained shimmer suggested a proscenium. Desperate to escape the stifling parochialism, he'd always seen the world as his stage, but standing at the threshold he felt an hermetic pressure sucking him towards his destiny.

As the forest thickened it disappeared, then flared as it reemerged. The sentinels were relieved to see the apparition scramble down the embankment to the path and rest its lantern on the dry stone wall before clambering over. Flesh and blood.

Tom released his grip on James' musket and, still transfixed, fumbled behind for his own. James' trembling finger rattled the trigger, but as it came within range, he realised he couldn't fire. So this was what they meant by 'frozen with fear'. But no, not fear - anticipation...awe. Though he knew he need not shoot, his gun remained poised. The figure approached undeterred, stopped about ten yards away and placed the lantern down. As he stepped forward, limbs outstretched in unarmed innocence, his silhouette split the beam and shafts corona-ed into the night.

James' hands stopped trembling. He felt a warmth and half turned to see if Tom had neared with the torch. Even without the lantern the figure remained suffused with illumination. He seemed to be emanating light.

James fully intended to say – "Halt! Stranger" but by the time he opened his mouth its guarded confrontation had dissolved into – "Welcome friend".

As his vision adjusted he could see the man was smiling. A gentle smile, so devoid of challenge, so inviting, that James found himself smiling back. Several minutes later he and Tom were shaking their heads, dizzied, embarrassed, and a foreign body had violated the village quarantine.

"What should we do?" asked James

"What would Bull do?" said Tom.

Maybe the heavens hadn't collapsed, but something had dropped to the earth. The sky hadn't fallen in, but someone, had to go tell the king.

Round an' a Round

It starts like this: a beer, another beer, a beer and whisky chaser, breakfast. Beer, port, beer, gin, beer, rum, beer. It starts like this, and ends when a bloated corpse is fished out of the dock.

Round an' a round. He'd watched it since sunrise now. Beautiful in a way, relaxing, bobbing beneath the beams, one way then another, clockwise then counter, so peaceful, sending ripples out to sea against the tide. It reemerged from under the jetty and this time he hit it, spat a long lazy line of dirty brown tobacco juice across its back with a satisfying splash, and wondered again if he should piss on it.

He recognized the balding head, broad back and thought – what the fuck's Jimmy doing face down in the dock - but only with the same disinterest he felt for anything these days. Four people had died from the sickness in the last two weeks, one a young girl, and they were saying once you had it that was it. He'd never been an emotional man, but any sympathy he did have was dwindling.

Better send the boy for the sheriff…he spat, whittled some more…still, no hurry, there'd be no boats leaving this dock today. The fish had gone, the sea was dry, but unless something changed soon they'd be boxing the dead like cod.

Black magic, Satan's work, the Lord's wrath, whatever you called it, something had a grip on the village and he knew it wasn't gonna let go. He knew, not because he had some understanding of God's Will, but because there was no *God's Will*, just stuff that happened, and this was some of it. He'd been in enough sea storms to know there was no good and evil struggle, it was just nature doing its business and sometimes you had to baton down the hatches and sit it out. Let them ration their crops, raise their committees, say their prayers and send out their search parties - only killing time before the inevitable. There was nothing he could do, and he was doing it the best he could.

Alcohol poisoning? Bob threw back another shot and made the sign of the cross. Dead before he hit the dock? He didn't know how they figured these things out – the red face? The discolouration of the lips? The 40 years of alcohol abuse? - and he didn't care, either way he was standing in The Long Bar, half drunk, wearing his brother's best shirt and Jimmy Johnston was lying on the bar in a box. Thirty six inverted shot glasses lay alongside the coffin - early tributes from mourners who couldn't bear a sober ceremony - and by dusk there would be over a hundred more.

Round an' a round an' a round...then a piss and another round. As teenagers he and Jimmy set off on a head-spinning quest that saw their gang reel around the taverns every Thursday, Friday, Saturday night without fail, and (funds provided) Sunday afternoon too. But what began as a celebratory romp became a centrifugal carousal that separated the men from the boys. The day his dad's death left him sole breadwinner was the day Bob side-stepped into manhood, but Jimmy continued his adolescence with abandon. Drinking became part of his identity...then it became all of his identity. When he couldn't make it to the Quay, the Mill, the Market, or countless other lost jobs, on Monday mornings if it meant passing an alehouse, it had started to spiral out of control. It whipped into a whirl of misadventure – self-destructive antics and casual vandalism as they tried to out derring-do each other - then descended into a dark vortex of brinkmanship. As they battled to cultivate their dysfunction and celebrate their rage, the moral boundaries blurred then vanished.

Between late teens and early twenties, between opening time and dawn, Jimmy discovered a pocket of stillness, in the back room of The Fleece, and a talent as a comic storyteller.

'One of me earliest memories was fetchin me dad from The Long Bar - standin in the doorway, thrilled and sickened by tha warm beery smell, watching the men laugh and sing songs in the shadas of the back room. By the time ar'd walked the lengtha the bar ar was dizzy on the fumes. Me da 'ad left the ouse in a door-slammin rage, now 'e and Bobby Armstrong were roarin an backslappin...and drinkin. What was that stuff? A coupla years later me and Nine Eyes noticed the back gate to the Fleece was open, snook inter the yard, nicked

a crate a' ale and drank it down the Black Sands. Ar' was eight years auld.

That was good, lyin there in the dunes, 'ead spinnin, laughin and vomitin, but ther' was summit missin - the ale'ouse. Me da rarely drank at 'ome, but then 'e never 'ad the chance - 'e was always in tha fuckin' Longbar. After that, so was ar - right there whenever me Ma wanted 'im 'ome for 'is tea! Sneakin through the tables suppin dregs and cadgin' mouthfuls from fat men who'd chase me through the cheers shoutin 'just like 'is fuckin' da', when ar downed their pint in one.'

For several glorious years he conjured up good feeling where before there was none, spreading bonhomie with anecdotes and jokes. He attracted an entourage of curious drinkers who'd come from all over town to witness his routine and test his drinking prowess. He sat, with a cynical amusement, at the eye of the storm, calling for another round while the social world of the village revolved around him.

Scandinavian fishermen would come off the boats to buy him a drink and attempt to dethrone him, but Jimmy, his patter sovereignty in the battle for conversational territory, was majestic. Power corrupts they say, and several gallons of alcohol will mess with your head too. What once loosened his tongue began to tighten its grip, strangulating his wit and cutting off the circulation to his judgment. No one had questioned his drinking when he seemed happy, he was someone who 'really knows how to enjoy himself', but as it began to curdle he became someone who —' doesn't know when to stop'.

Occasionally Bob would see him in the back room on a weekend and make some casual crack about his excessive drinking. Jimmy would just shrug and give one of his usual quips: "I've got a big appetite for life, and I need something to wash it down with." But it wasn't quenching his thirst for life, it was gradually extinguishing it.

He became bitter, abusing drinkers with scathing attacks. And when he'd succeeded in alienating strangers, he set about reducing his friends to a vicious circle of sado-masochistic thugs who enjoyed the give and take of savage beatings. When he lost the ability to form coherent insults it was a blessing that probably saved him from a fatal retaliation.

He would be drunk when he woke up. Bob was passing the market one morning when he overheard him haranguing Paddy the butcher about the pronunciation of his name – 'No - Jhimmy John-shton. Not John-shon. Jimmy John-John-John-shton' – slurring his words into further confusion.

He became a joke, a laughing stock. Gradually barred from pub after pub, you'd find him on the beach drinking gin oblivious to the kids singing taunts and throwing stones at him. His wife Annie petitioned the landlords until only Alfie in The Grill (an out of towner) would serve him. Jimmy sat in the alcove beneath the window mumbling about injustice - like Napoleon in Exile, 'cept with shit streaked down the back of his trouser legs.

It stripped him of everything he had, everything he loved and everything he was, sucked the lifeblood from his veins and replaced it with poisonous momentum that drove him, compelled him to lie, cheat and steal to perpetuate his dehumanizing daily routine. Take away his pint and he was barely there, just an absence in a cap. So sad that a life built on celebration and good humour should end in dereliction and seclusion. He had painted himself into a corner.

When Bob worked in the tannery he would see him ambling down the street on a morning and think of Mitchell's dog that would run around the house rubbing its head against the wall. His wife wanted an exorcism, but Mitchell had it shot.

Jimmy's gyrations cut him a rut that consisted of the walk – about 138 steps on the way there, more scenic and circuitous on the way home – from his house to The Fleece and then dug him a six foot hole in St Hild's Church yard.

Bob dragged a stool into the middle of the crowd. It was a sad reflection of Jimmy's decline, that though they hadn't drank together for over 20 years, it was decided he should deliver the eulogy.

"No one's gonna start white washin' the past. We all know Jimmy 'ad 'is problems and there'll be few in 'ere who haven' been tortured by 'im at some point over the last 10 years. But, an we can see by the turn out today, there's also few who 'aven sat in the corner of The Ship or The Fleece when 'e 'eld court and listened to 'is jokes an stories, or enjoyed a lock-in when 'e wouldn't let ye pay for a round. The older generation know him not as the fat drunk who sat on the Fish Sands, but as the life and soul of the village. There was a time when if you walked into a tavern and 'e was there you wouldn wanna leave in

56

case ye missed summit.

"'e was an artist – Aye, a piss artist! I 'ear you cry…but in a town like this, is there any better kind? They uste come from all over to buy 'im a drink and listen to his bullshit – the Dutch and the Norwegians – an 'ed sup 'em under the table. Ar remember the 'ush that fell over the pub when that arrogant bastard from Whitechapel sa' down without a word nexte Jimmy with two bottles a gin…and I also remember the roar just after two o'clock when the fat cunt shook the dust off the Ship's floorboards.

"'is palate was 'is patter, and maybe if he'd chosen the campfire instead of the barstool he would still be spinning 'em on the beach today.

"So yeh, he was a piss artist…one of the best," he raised his glass in the air "AN 'E WAS OUR PISS ARTIST!" He saw his drink off in one and everyone in the room did likewise.

"Now ar want everyone to join me in a minute's silence."

Bob bowed his head and placed his hands on his lap.

"Ar want everyone to cast ther minds back and remember a 'appier time, remember a positive moment, the' spent with Jimmy."

"I remember one Saturda' we wer in the Globe, first pint of an all dayer, we'r havin' a piss out the back an' 'e starts chucklin' to 'imself. 'Wha ye laughin' at?' I said. 'Arm just wonderin'' 'e sez, "who's turn it is t'give me a good hidin' today?"'.

"Remember when Little Paddy and Brian and them went drinking in Cranleigh and came back bloodied. Jimmy wanted to get a mob together, go through in carts and kick the shit outta them – 'C'mon' he sez 'we'll take some beers and a picnic, make a real day of it'. He was dead serious an all."

"…when he worked down the Quay with Sammy Stokes, he brought that bag of live crabs into the Grill and fought them in the yard…he had to take all the dead crabs home for the bairns to eat because Shaw won all his wages off him!"

"Ye remember when he stuck his finger up that dog's arse!"

57

Oh they had plenty to say now, she thought, but where were they when he fuckin' needed them? For year's they bowed their 'eads as they passed 'im in the corner an no-one said a bastard word. He was a shadow, a ghost, and they were waiting for him to die. 'Ye can't interfere with a man's business', they'd say, and watched him disintegrate rather than break that unspoken code.

'There's nowt ye can do Annie,' they said. ''e 'as te want te stop 'imself' they said. That's what they said, and that's what she heard when she looked around for help. So final, so inevitable. Annie didn't believe in destiny – just fuckin' laziness, cowardice, to blame destiny.

They were gonna do this now! Fuckers!

It wasn't the grief that made Annie bitter, she'd lost him long ago. No one could explain it. At the end they were all waiting for him to die. He haunted their lives, no one knew how he'd hung on for so long.

Bob the Dog had stuck by him as long as he could. He was a good man, a good man. But he had six kids to look after. What she couldn't understand was how they could go about with their lives without doing anything. Why didn't they all just stop – his ma, his brothers, his sister, his aunties and uncles, his cousins, his workmates, his friends, go down the Grill and drag him out. But it wasn't done. His brothers just said: "Annie, we've talked to 'im Annie, we all 'ave. Arve said everything ar can – arve got nowt else to say."

"It's in the blood" – that was more of the bullshit that meant his lazy brothers didn't have to get off their arses and help her. Just because their auld man was a drunkard, Jimmy had to go the same way – like he had an excuse, a right, an expectation.

And now it was her who had to raise those kids singlehanded, scrubbing floors at the brewery, blistering up her fingers mending nets. She worked three jobs to feed them kids and she'd beat the shit out of Little Geordie when money went missing from her jar beneath the floorboards – the first time it happened. Only later she realized who she'd have to hide her wages from, and the household things, and the bairns' clothes. Ask them what they thought of the World's Greatest Pisshead - they'd rather have had a dad.

Round an' a round an' a round. Her thoughts, always returning to the same

58

place. She stood up to go for a shit and her head spun – she was a bit pissed.

So the afternoon unfolded into oblivion and the evening and morning followed. Jimmy's misadventures passed into legend and no one said:

"Remember when their Jack nearly died o' pneumonia and 'e was too pissed te care. On 'is death bed they thought, his own brother, and Jimmy didn't budge from the Grill."

And Bob's most enduring memory - of Jimmy slumped one Sunday afternoon over a glass of gin, more coughed up more blood than liquor – also went unmentioned, as did the times Albert's missus had to scrub shit and vomit from Jimmy's corner. And no one said:

"Ye remember when he drank so much 'is respiratory system and blood circulation ceased to function and 'e stopped breathin?"

The town was in despair, one of its oldest sons had passed away - a happy ending needed to be fashioned from the unlikely material of death, and somehow it was.

"'ere's te you Jimmy. Ye liked to see 'ow far ye could go – well now ye know!"

The Caul

A baleful thump. A dull thud thud. The seaman's wife, the touch of wood. She stopped mid-fold and laid her palm like a steadying prayer – 'oh please Lord' - the cold kitchen table the other half of her supplication, her ballast, her anchor.

Between the idea and the reality, between the first knock and the last, lay a gravid pause in which a death was born. His life flashed before her eyes, more absence than presence - coming and going, ebbing and flowing - he was out more than the tide. The sea could be a cruel mistress they said – and a cheap whore! Storms, tides, pirates, scaly eight armed beasts, all conspired to keep him at sea and somehow send him back drunk.

The excuses, she'd heard them all over the years, but this was the last, the best, the ultimate and she'd never get to hear it, because she knew, just knew (same as last time and the time before) that he'd never come home again.

He could hear the sirens' song.

He closed his eyes, tapped his heel on the mast and made a silent prayer. He'd be working salt-horse for a week or two if the wind didn't pick up. He didn't mind the stringy meat but he was damned if he'd walk into Rotterdam without a pocketful of guilders - there was no slate in that town, and only one bait got them biting.

But he'd been caught last time. He walked out of there penniless, and then around for three days in a dream. When he awoke his money was gone, but whatever that girl put in his drink, would always be there. Maybe always had.

She didn't understand, coming home from church with His words in her mouth. Depravity they called it. Total depravity. He shouted her down, gave her a few smacks, but it was true, when the nets were all in then his thoughts turned to sin – it was what he had to do.

He could hear the sirens' song - his name a refrain.

He was always destined to leave, but he didn't know until he'd left that he was destined to return.

Did the scripture not say - 'the kingdom of heaven is as a man travelling into a far country' and if he was to embark on this quest then where better than the Holy Lands? But when the muezzin sang from the minarets his mind turned to the St Hild bells.

Vocatio specialis. He heard it. Like a divine request - God's irresistible grace urging him to pilgrimage...he thought. Now he asked himself - was the voice, reduced to a whisper beneath a barrage of fear and doubt, inside or out? The scripture also said - 'cast ye the unprofitable servant into outer darkness'.

He'd been cast - like bread upon waters, from post to pillar, aside like a thorn, and for what? He'd returned now to help his home town and they treated him like a stranger. He had one chance, an old friend who he hoped could forgive the vanity of youth. He'd taken pride in his passion, his mission, been seduced by the idea of destiny. 'Greatness' they'd said - all because of that thin translucent skin covering the top of his head. 'Like a little hat,' they said 'or a crown...or a halo.'

Put a sea shell to your ear, they said, and you could hear the roar and shush of the ocean. The sea was in his blood, his bones, his head and that's what he heard when he held up a conch. No, what he needed was a reminder of land. He crossed himself and there she was resonating in his breast pocket, over his heart - 'ye may think yer an auld sea dog, but don't forget which corners ye pissed in!'

She came home from church, he never asked where she got it, just refused to carry it. It wasn't natural. They had a huge row, a change from the one about him being baptised. He only agreed when she told him the price. I could sell it he'd thought...and yet there it was, impossibly, pressed onto paper.

He didn't believe in its protective properties anyway, but when he touched it he heard her voice reminding him to be careful and smiled at her faith keeping him safe through his cynicism.

The haddock is easily recognized by a black lateral line running along its white side, not to be confused with the pollock which has the reverse – a white line on a black side.

Bull was no fisherman. He'd worked the boats for the opportunities. 'Catch men like fish' Jesus told his disciples. Nothing would be wasted. Throw the fish guts onto your garden crops they said, but he fed them to stray cats.

He took another fish from the bucket. It squirmed and he tightened his grip. If you press a fish's eyes it paralyses it they said. He pressed the fish's eyes. He didn't have to cut them up. He didn't have to get his hands dirty. He could leave that to the boys now, they had a talent for it.

He sliced the fish along the belly - this was how they told the future, the shamen, the seers, reading the omens in guts - and tipped the innards into a bucket. He knew the future. Could see it so strongly, like it had already happened.

Didn't they say he'd been born inside the sack, that it was so rare it meant he was destined for greatness? That dark blotch above the haddock's fin - St. Peter's Mark they called it, or some, the Devil's Thumbprint. He still had the forehead scars where it had been badly removed.

The one thing his mother had left with the old woman and he'd sold it. It might seem wrong now, but they would proclaim his righteousness to those yet unborn.

They threw him the rope, repeatedly, but no matter how close he just couldn't grab it. They watched helpless as he was caught in a current, spun in a vortex, body submerged, one straight arm holding a fold of paper sticking out of the whorl. Salvation doesn't call on us all.

Auto-da-fe (or Never Boil a Scapegoat in its Mother's Milk)

Not far away lies a deep dark forest, and in it stands a crooked little hut, and in that hut lives a strange little man, and every night that little man eats a bowl of fish and potato stew, says a prayer for his dear dead mother and goes to bed early — except tonight, because tonight his house is on fire.

The bastard son of a gypsy dancer and a bare knuckle boxer, like his encampment birthplace that straddled the old town wall border, Billy's nature had always been split. His da, a native Crofter, juggled trawling and drinking with fucking and fighting - a work/life imbalance that meant his women weren't complaining when it came to his leaving. For eight months Billy's mother endured the beatings until his father's blood called him back to sea. By then his mother, keen to her firstborn's needs, had settled in the Romani camp on the outskirts of town. She'd made many friends in the Croft, and when her husband succumbed to his nomadic tendencies she found it surprisingly easy to resist her own ('just in case I bump into him').

She came from farming stock and had always made extra money telling fortunes and treating ailments with herbs. 'Half o' the land, half o' the sea/Will he a fisherman or a farmer be' his grandma sang before she died. After she did, his mother would hum the tune, wondering when he, like his four step-brothers, would head out to sea; or hitch up to a passing caravan like his uncles. But, by boyhood, Billy's nature became much more unpredictable than the mesh of his mongrel kinfolk, and his options less than twofold.

Some say his mother was cursed

Some say his father was his brother

Some say he was kicked by a horse

Some say he drank too much sea water

Some say his step-brothers did unspeakable things

But everyone agreed that, although he'd spent twenty six years in a two roomed shack with his beloved mother and a flea-bitten wolfhound, there was a vacancy in Billy that reflected his heritage.

Water from the well, water from the well – for 20 years his mother worked tirelessly to counteract her son's simple mindedness, setting repetitive tasks to sustain him after she'd gone. She taught him how to feed the chickens with a ponderous attention and apply wood ash to the onion beds. They made so many trips to market Billy could eventually do it alone; but if anyone stopped him to discuss weather or his mother's health he'd shake his head side to side and moan the tune that earned him his nickname – La La.

Billy survived thanks to the watchful eyes of his mother's friends, but no matter how many times his 'Auntie' Ann told him the fish were all gone, the next day would find him standing forlorn in the deserted Market Square waiting to trade with eggs and turnips.

Livestock long gone, horse meat next. Some chickens survived but their owners lived in fear. They were living on corn and veg, and alcohol had supplanted meals as the main source of calories. You could meet an old friend on the street and he'd be gaunt from malnutrition but half drunk.

Tensions simmered. The town bubbled like a cauldron. There'd been another victim, just yesterday, a little girl, only four years old, had gone missing from her home, and it was largely assumed the sickness had taken her. The guards' tale spread, and Bull, sure the stranger was carrying the virus, convinced the parish council he must be found. A rumour had spread connecting him to the child's disappearance, and a reward was offered for his capture.

"So?"

"Wha?"

"Ye expect me t' sit 'ere all night wi' you two cunts when all the drink 'as gone. Ar' we gonna do it or not?"

Caleb took a swig of gin and cursed under his breath, bile scalding his throat. He was too angry to feel intoxicated, but determined to get his share. Almost two thirds of his money and those bastards had snook off and bought it while he was still at the mill. The cheap liquor was potent, the transgressive thrill of black market dealings - heady. So Jack and Paddy were already giggly, teasing Caleb for his sobriety.

They argued and he wrestled with Jack for the bottle but big Paddy had knocked him down– 'you'll get ya share Caleb – don't spoil it for everyone now'. The threat was tacit but tangible. Now they sat round a beach fire passing the bottle, and with each huddled joke *they* shared Caleb imagined beating Paddy to a pulp.

"Wha' if 'e's innocent?" he said, deciding reason was the most objectionable element he could introduce to the conversation.

"Innocent! 'Ow can 'e be innocent? Said Paddy. "'E's so fuckin' crazy 'e could do it without even knowin'. Innocent…" He chucked a stick into the fire. "'e's guilty of summit!"

"Anyway, even if 'im didn' take the little girl 'im doesn' belong 'ere. 'E's not a true Crofter. 'Es never fitted in" said Jack.

"Well, 'e was born 'ere" said Caleb.

"Those fuckin' gypos should never have come round 'ere, takin' our jobs."

"Well Paddy, there's been gypsies up on the Kop for over a 'undred years, and your granddad only came over from Ireland when ya ma was a bairn."

"Yeh, but my fuckin' grandmother wasn't a witch was she!?"

"Oh, ye believe in witches now do ye?"

"My granddad said they wanted t' string 'er up when the gypos got 'ere, 'im said they woulda done in his day, but now there's a law" said Jack.

"Aye" said Paddy. "I worked wi Byers in the slaughterhouse a few years ago, an 'e told me 'is son got stung by a jelly fish when 'e was swimmin' by the jetty, an 'is neck swole up like a pig and 'e went all cold and stiff. They took 'im up t' 'er and she sang a song and rubbed leafs on his chest."

"So now you wanna run her son out of town because she saved ye friend's lad's life?"

Caleb watched the cogs, like the millwheel on a morning, turning slowly behind the ignorance. He waited until he thought Paddy hadn't heard him, and just as he was about to repeat himself the big Irishman said: "Well, I'm not gonna sit around wi' you two cunts when all the drink 'as gone."

If Paddy could have articulated his feelings he might have said that he couldn't bear to feel impotent, and that he'd rather be wrong than have to sit still and think for another moment. They were in desperate need of a crusade, but a lynching would have to do.

Scorched earth and gravel, the gypsies chopped down trees and burnt clearings for their caravans. Though they lived on the outskirts of town, their exoticism bewitched the more adventurous Crofters who would sneak up at night to celebrate. Of course when the borders were eventually redrawn to incorporate their camp the justification cited was imported goods, with no mention of their principle commodity - women.

The deflowering of daughters was a continual conflict, and though bare knuckle fights were commonplace the violence was only comparable to that which the Crofters meted out on each other. Occasionally a close knit gypsy family would successfully force an unwanted union onto a hapless Crofter – hence Billy's brief period with a full filial complement.

The bottle exploded and the thatched roof went up like a scream. Caleb glanced at their faces, aglow with orange shock, and smiled. They'd trod on the vegetable patch, smashed the chicken coop, thrown stones at the windows, but he'd gone one better. High on adrenaline, bent on revenge, he'd built a makeshift bomb from the rag and the gin. His rage exorcised in one cathartic act. That'll teach them to fuck with him.

Billy was sat on the edge of his bed counting. He stood up, pushed in his chair, sat wedged between the wall and the stove and rocked back and forth humming.

So beautiful. Red, orange, yellow, white - the most light he'd seen for weeks - danced against the night. The flames, violent, invigorating, It seemed like the perfect way to deal with all this injustice – burn it down.

The smoke billowed into huge columns, like cauliflowers, or mushrooms. He could feel the warmth pleasant on his face, the smell of charcoal and he put out his hand as ash fluttered down like black snow.

"You *stupid* cunt! We were only suppose to fuckin' scare 'im." Paddy began distancing himself from blame. Jack had a better technique - he ran off into the woods...with Paddy two steps behind.

Caleb wanted to run but he couldn't. He was transfixed. He was shocked by his own success. With percolating clarity he saw the scene for the first time – the cottage was on fire...and there was a man inside! Oh God!

It wasn't even his idea, it was *them two*. *Them two* with their whispering and their laughing, hogging the gin on the way up the hill. That was his fuckin money and...Oh God!

Maybe it was okay. Surely with the sickness no one was gonna miss one re-tarded gypsy. Maybe he would escape punishment, but he knew, now, as panic pulsed through his brain – Oh God! Why doesn't he run out! – that restitution lay not with the town parish.

That smell, sulfur. The fumes. Choking. The heat. His skin blistered. So much smoke. Vast, belching gas and ash, black billowing waste, and in the middle of all that angry combustion Caleb fancied he saw shapes in the abstractions. A demon rising, charred and fiery, towering up with huge, clawed hands, reaching down to take him by the throat. He had sinned. He had flirted with evil and now he must suffer God's wrath, a tempest of snares, fire and brimstone would rain down in judgment, and he would be tormented day and night forever and ever. Damnation.

He coughed. Poison. Blood in his throat. His chest tightened. His knees buckled. He staggered, blacked out and vomited. He spat, clearing the bilious taste from his mouth, took a few steps back and fell to his knees. A high pitched whine, a piercing shriek. His? Billy's? He crouched into a ball and wrapped his arms around his head to ward off the burgeoning screams. Conflict. Abrasion.

Two sides of his brain shifted against each other like tectonic plates. Oh God, help me. Then there was a snap and a massive release of tension.

When he looked up the demon was gone, the black smoke had cleared and in its place he saw an angel ascending, ascending, proud, majestic, magnificent, liberated, happy, enlightened, ascending to heaven, all corporeal troubles dissolving, finally leaving this Godforsaken place forever.

That's the way Caleb saw it, but to the naked eye it looked more like a man burning to death.

Whisper Down The Lane

Listen. There's something going around.

Aye Alfie, get me another/I swear she did, and ye never 'eard owt?/yee as well... scruffy seacole 'awkers/that's more than enough/Ar've been down for 10 minutes man!/How would ye know?/woudn' 'ear a werd/Drink it up/Always in the pawnbrokers...next stop alehouse, ha ha ha!/the state of it, ye wouldn't would ye?/Eeee, never/. 'Ere, watch where you're putting ye bloody 'ands/Ye lyin' bastard!...

An ill wind is blowing through the land, carrying things it shouldn't carry mouth to mouth, ear to ear. Whiping down the alleyways, stirring rubbish and rumour in dark corners. Sea coal ashes, rotten fish, dead rats, rag, shit, sand and patter, tamped down by heavy boots and poverty. The essence of Crofters, laminated debris dumped in the thin seams behind the backs of cramped dwellings. The Lanes were densely packed slums, a breeding ground for dirt, disease and young mothers selling themselves to feed their kids or habits.

On the edge of those slums was The Pot House, build so close to the sands that when the planets conspired, when the moon was full and new, drinkers could be found supping ale ankle deep in spring tides. No matter, for these hardcore boozers were in it up to their eyebrows: beery high water marks tattooed on their brains.

Most mornings you'd find Cissie Hunter earning a modest living from crabs, but recently her shellfish trade had been supplanted by homemade grog. An offer of cheap rum had turned her home - ropes and nets still hung from the walls - into a makeshift ale house. Bill pushed a table up beneath the window moved the bairns into the smaller, damper room and prayed for health.

The sickness was among them, but for many, life went on as usual. No one was really sure how you got it, though they'd heard the travellers' tales. Fishwives traded stories scrubbing clothes in the yard - 'I 'eard ye burn pepper te ward it off' - 'No, no, no - ye put *snails* in yer mouth' — more in curiosity than fear. With all the cloud they were enjoying late autumn warmth and liquor. Some, were even a little excited, drunk on the disruption to their daily grind, while others, were drunk on moonshine.

Cissie's was packed. The rum was a welcome alternative to the cheap gin, attracting many who usually avoided The Lanes' undertow of illicit sex and violence. Most of the fishermen had given up trawling, sold their last catch and, as the grey skies thickened into evening, were half way through the proceeds.

An absurdist circus spilled into the yard. Drunks performed elaborate waltzes - sometimes with partner, sometimes without - while a crowd clapped and stamped their feet. The bairns ran up and down the sands or sat on the steps laughing at the antics. An old man slumped in a corner, wearing a jacket but no shirt, was weeping and a woman began cursing an invisible foe in what sounded like a foreign tongue. The crowd started up a sea shanty.

'When the nets are all in... hahahahaha get him then, get him... then my thoughts turn to sin... whhhyyy Maggie, whhhyyy did you dooo that to me!..we set sail... You're not funny, you're not funny, you're NOT FUCKIN' FUNNY...for a bit of a spree, boys, set sail for a bit of a spree.'

Amidst the drunken roil that day was a whisper that would soon resound above the revelry. They'd agreed, Tom and James, when they'd regained their senses, that they need not mention it - not to Bull, not to anyone. But they were wrong, because at that moment, on different sides of the packed pub they were simultaneously suppressing the urge to confess.

It was like shit or vomit thought James, he couldn't relax till it was out of his system. He'd been struggling ever since they vowed to keep stumm. He knew they'd experienced something phenomenal, been touched by a force they couldn't understand and he had to share it. He leant right into Sally's ear, opened his mouth and...he had no idea how to start, not even the first word, not even the basic components of a sentence. How could he explain it...and yet...he tried again...no. He wanted to tell her he'd enjoyed an incredible, beautiful, uplifting, invigorating experience, an ecstasy, a rapture, an intense wave of love and that he would never be the same again. But even if this vocabulary had been available to James, it would have been impossible to communicate in such an indifferent climate.

Tom didn't know what had happened, but he knew it wasn't drinkin', fuckin' or fightin', so it didn't belong in the pub. He didn't want to think about it, he just wanted to fulfill his promise to James to 'get rat-arsed down Cissie's', but he'd already drank half a bottle of rum and was still annoyingly sober. He wished it hadn't happened, he wished he'd never been there, he wished his guts weren't aching. He couldn't stop thinking about it.

Why had she let him drag her down there? She was respectable...she knew people, she couldn't be seen frequenting such lousy piss-holes. The place was filthy, full of drunks and whores. Honestly, some of the company he kept...so fuckin' vulgar. She tried to keep her good skirt out of the puddles. 'I'll take you out' he says...Sometimes she thought her ma was right. 'Sometimes I think me ma was right!' she shouted forlornly because James was gazing across the room with a faraway look in his eye.

He'd been thinking about Tom ever since they parted. He felt an incredible connection, an affinity he'd never known before, and when he saw him come in he had to resist the need to go over, embrace him and discuss it in depth. They were linked now, bound – but where?

'Five, shix...five, shix...five, shix, sheven...ere, Tom, Shid, Ellis...lend ush shome money wil ye?' A series of savage beatings had left Sonny Elliott with minimal teeth, a broken nose and a comical speech impediment...which just seemed to provoke more fights. He was trying to calculate if he had enough money for a bottle and a whore, but was too drunk to count.

He was gibbering, gabbling, because he'd been out all day, because he hated silence, because he wanted something instead of nothing, because he feared he was a tragic shell of a man who barely existed unless he was amidst some self-inflicted melodrama. He needed something to fill the emptiness – drink? sex?...if he couldn't get the money he was going to belt someone.

Suddenly voices and tension were raised, shouts and gesticulations over by the door. His drunken mates jostled for conversational territory, but in the

73

midst of the melee Tom wore the beatific smile of the recently unburdened.

James craned his neck without luck because, unlike his friends, Tom was speaking in a measured, gentle, tone. He'd uttered a phrase of devastating syllables in the slightest of decibels – a confession of sorts, though he felt no shame, just serenity.

As the accusations heated and the fingers jabbed, Sonny Elliot elbowed his way through to the front. James knew Elliot – he was the main reason he refused to drink with Tom's crowd; a vicious little bastard who wouldn't let sentimentality spoil the thrill of a double hanging.

He could see it all spread, like the spider veins in his mother's legs - Sonny Elliot was knocking off Lily Tucker, a friend of Carol Bancroft, who was seeing Matty Stewart who used to work in Fuller's Field up by the Old Windmill with Mick Houghton who was now seeing Polly Horsley. Polly Horsley's daughter Kitty had been seen on the Town Wall with Ferret McKinley who drank with Geordie Roberson, Ken Stout and Philly Smee, who was fucking Ginny Keane behind Buck's back. He could see it all spread, passed around the incestuous mess like a dose of syphilis.

They knew.

Vicious sibilances hissed in his peripheries, mumbled slanders inventoried his sins. He couldn't hear their words but he could feel their contempt – *e's the one/e's the one/learnin te read/who des 'e think 'e is/e's the one/e's the one.* He felt faint. He closed his eyes. An image flashed across his mind - a snake coiled consuming its tail - so vividly he was shaken. He eyed them slyly waiting for a hand on his shoulder, or worse.

'Fine fuckin gentlemen *you* turned out to be. *Ar ye gonna get me a drink or wha?*'

Nervous he spun and knocked over some jars. Again, a portentous vision – pitchforks, torches, a conflagration, corpses bonfired, charred limbs at unholy angles, brimstone, devils, decay.

They were dead.

Sally called after him as he pushed through the crowd. He needed fresh air

- there was none. Outside, dizzy he tried to steady himself against a coble and almost swooned. The drunks were singing an old folk round and the bairns had joined in with their nursery rhymes. Oaths, curses, sermons, blasphemy - it all spiraled up in his head as he staggered off down an alleyway.

Ee's the one/ 'e's the one/learnin' te read/e's the one/cunt! cunt! don' cum back!/who des e think e is/ring a-ring o' roses/cunt! cunt!/A pocketful of posies/ cunt!/atishoo! atishoo/We all fall down.

Reconciliation

By day the devout descended. Self-flagellation was forbidden in the churchyard, but a trail of blood and skin crawled up the Market Street cobbles to the steps. Self-proclaimed sinners genuflecting in the pews from dawn till dusk begging the Lord for mercy.

At night the heretics shifted behind the headstones, decapitating statues, smashing the stained glass and torching the undergrowth while Father John crouched behind rectory window boards, clutching his Bible and wondering why his faith didn't convert into courage.

The priest rose early to open the church, but already a blanket clad figure knelt outside the doors finishing her seventh decade of rosaries. Pain shot through Maggie's old bones, prompting a mix of grimace and smile. It wasn't enough. Both her children had the sickness. Three days ago huge black boils had appeared in David's armpits and the next day Anne's lips began to grey. The church was being repaired after an arson attack, but as soon as it reopened she'd lit them a benedictory candle, and now the Lord was punishing her by taking her baby daughter. Why, why, had she said David's name first? She would never forgive herself. She held her cloak tight with one hand and counted out beads with the other. Her prayer never missed a beat - "Sanctus Sanctus…Benedictus. Sanctus Sanctus…Benedictus." – as Father John took her under the arm and guided her gently into the church.

Simple minded idiots. Queuing outside the confession box. Who could confide in this man – this small, insignificant man? Hidebound by faith, predictable, pious, transparent. Bull could read him like a book - The Good Book. *This* is where they came for salvation – from a man who couldn't think without looking it up first, who couldn't act without consulting his boss.

Bull suffered no such restrictions. Morality? Guilt? Conscience? He'd squared that with the Lord a long time ago. They'd discussed it, come to an agreement and now he was free to pursue his destiny. That's how he could be surrounded by death and recognise it as opportunity; that's why he'd used curfew to smuggle liquor up the beach, that's why, despite their misguided protests, he'd made *sure* the Bridge was safe.

He'd saved them, but they would never know it. He almost pitied them… but pity wasn't his business - let God get on with it. There would always be winners and losers – that's just the way things were, the way they'd always be, and when this sickness had passed through town and flushed out the weak, he would be stronger than ever. And now he'd have to save them again, because if he left it to this fool he'd lose all his custom to St Peter.

Bull's communion was a private matter, but he needed to consult the pastor and it served his purposes to be seen in church. He stepped in front of the queue and the crowd shuffled and lowered their heads. Someone at the back shouted and then noticing, retreated into the shadows mumbling. Laying his head casually against the stanchion Bull knocked on the listening door.

In the middle of penance? Who would be so disrespectful? Leaning out of the box Father John bridled when he saw Bull – smiling – and the power of jurisdiction switched allegiances. Though he'd been expecting this since The Bridge netting he was still ill-prepared. Everything sped up. His mind raced through the complex machinations and sly self-deceptions needed to deal with the man. Something bordering on hatred had to be suppressed until it untroubled his consciousness or affected his righteousness.

He ducked back inside to retrieve his crosier and took a moment to cross himself and ask the Lord for strength. In straitened times he felt, the pageantry was even more important - hence the staff - but as he stepped out shakily he was grateful for the physical support.

No one could unnerve him like Henderson. He carried such a powerful negative presence - a charisma? an aura? a darkness?…Father John recoiled from that word – Evil. He'd seen too many hell fire sermonisers to believe in such Manichean rhetoric. That was the same medieval thinking that saw those poor souls thrash themselves through the streets. No, the fault was his. If his faith had been strong, Bull's intimidation would be powerless. But those eyes – so black and cold. He couldn't hold his gaze for more than a moment. He'd seen men slice into their foreheads, women deliberately burn their breasts. He'd once seen a man disembowelled, so why couldn't he look Bull in the eye?

Bull put a patronizing arm around Father John's shoulder and led him away to a corner. He looked back furtively at the queue. "Father I need a favour".

When they played brag in The Grill, Byers would flush with a pair, Stubbs twitched when he bluffed. Every man had something that gave him away - Father John had a handful.

"Whar I need from you Father is a blessin'. Like when you blessed The Bridge with the 'oly water and asked God te protect us. Lovely speech Father, really, ar was moved." He let his blandishment hang. He could feel the tension in the priest's shoulders and gait.

"But it didn't work! And now, as a result of that decision, in which you were instrumental, and te which, ar might remind ye, ar was strongly opposed - the village is in very, deep, shit."

As Father John remembered it the village had democratically decided to offer sanctuary to their neighbours, and Bull had seized control of security. Suspicious he thought, how so few afflicted had come a knocking since then. Then came rumours of a mysterious stranger who'd tricked his way past the guards. More intrigue. But all this clear thinking had been done before Bull arrived, now all he could think was – get him out of here!

"Now you and yer flock can continue te petition the Lord, that's great, but ar like to take a more… active approach. Ar need to catch 'im Father, we need to catch 'im. He's out there spreading death and disease. Nothing has entered since the nets went up, we saw te that, nothing except 'im. My men 'ave covered every inch of The Croft. E's got inside 'elp Father …someone's 'iding 'im."

As they talked they walked, Bull guiding the priest with his powerful left arm, and now as he brought him full circle back towards the confessional queue his entreaty became louder and more melodramatic.

"Because I made a promise. The day I stood out there and watched them bury the McCarty kid. As they lowered that little baby coffin into the ground, I vowed Father, vowed to his mother, that I would catch the man responsible.

"And I make another pledge Father, here and now" he looked up and saw the crowd, making sure they knew they were part of the show: "as God is my witness, I will not rest until I catch the man who has wreaked such devastation on the village I love."

Father John realized he was playing the pawn, but it was way down on his priorities list that started No 1. Get Him Out of Here! No 2. Get. Him. Out. Of. Here!

"And I came here today to ask, to plead, for your blessing Father. We've done all we can. Only one person can help us now." He cast his eyes to heaven "The people need to know that *He's* with us on this Father."

Continuing his circle as though it had all been incidental, Bull now turned Father John away from the queue and shifted the opera down an octave.

"They're 'arbourin' 'im Father, and ar want you te put a curse out there damnin' the culprits. Damnin' 'em to 'ell. Ar want everyone te know that whoever's protectin' this transgressor will be tortured for all eternity? Of course ye wone phrase it like that…well, you know what to do Father. We'll flush the bastard out."

He slapped the priest on the back, the ostensible gratitude buried beneath over familiar contempt.

"An if ye'll excuse me Father ar'll just go and ask a little forgiveness meself".

The priest closed his eyes in benediction - Please Lord no! Not this way, and when he opened them again Bull had passed the confessional box and was standing beneath the alter.

Bull crossed himself as he bowed his head, chuckling at his latest handy work. Contraband was hard, risky graft - he was in the wrong business. This preaching was easy money. He surprised himself sometimes. He'd had no idea what he was going to do until he did it - the spirit had just taken him.

He felt strong. The town was falling apart but for him it was all starting to come together. He was shifting liquor faster than they could ship it in. This plague had been the break he'd been waiting for, but he had to make sure it didn't get out of control. That's why he paid men to patrol the woods with extreme prejudice, that's why he'd captured six men, two women and three children, that's why he'd had them beheaded, their torsos and genitals hung in the trees outside town.

Now, bowed before Christ, Bull didn't ask forgiveness for this perdition. His sin was more original: "There are many in this town who wish to do me 'arm. Please Lord, watch over me and protect me from those who would seek to punish me for me crimes."

As his fear subsided Father John recovered a little indignation: 'I'm a man of God not some gypsy side show…the Lord cannot be bought or bullied', he proclaimed beneath the alter, but all he'd mustered in Bull's presence was a meek agreement that tomorrow he'd call a special service. But, this time, unlike his other capitulations he felt no humiliation, only relief. Just moments before Bull arrived he'd heard the confessional door shut, a familiar voice say – Bless me Father, it has been a while since my last confession - and knew this was one reconciliation Bull wouldn't absolve.

The One That Got Away

This was a town of fishermen, each time the arms got a little wider.

Ebb and flow, ebb and flow. He stood on the Town Wall watching the tide change, wondering how he'd been drawn back to the magnetic north. He'd escaped – driven by dreams, circled the globe and returned with fiery gifts – but no fatted calf awaited, not even a fried cod. The town was on starvation rations, but the rumour mill was churning. Stories are like children – feed them, they'll grow - but it was always the problem child who pushed to the front, shouting for more. They wanted more, they wanted a story to tell their grandchildren, a story that relieved the stifling mundanity of real life, a story that said these are exciting times and *I'm* living through them. There was a word for that kind of story, a word that followed him around, and he knew what it meant – trouble. Now it had been uttered like an imprecation and a spell had been cast.

Three days ago he'd been eating bread and wine in a tavern corner when the low moans of a girl drew him through the bar into a series of dank rooms. The moan faded but he followed the overwhelming smell of burning brimstone down a half flight of stone steps to ease the latch on a heavy door and enter soundlessly. Barrels in the corner, water running down the walls and a choking fug in what looked like a storage cellar. A woman sitting in a chair, holding a posy of tarragon lifted her head and, seeing him, stopped crying. He waded through the tobacco smoke and touched the shoulder of a man at the head of the bed who turned, puzzled holding a half-plucked pigeon in the girl's face.

He placed his hand on her brow and her heart rate slowed. He whispered in her ear and she stopped whimpering. He checked for lumps in her armpits, neck and groin. That's how he'd seen it in the Holy Land - growths in the pits, fingers and toe tips blackened, pestilence eating the flesh. But though the girl looked sickly, jaundiced, there were no symptoms. He recommended fresh water, made them promise to move the bed to a windowed room and no more (they'd been told it would ward off the bad air) smoldering brimstone.

As he left the tavern he dropped two ducats in a bowl of vinegar on the bar. Thirty-six hours later she was back on her feet, swabbing blood off the steps.

"They say she was not long f' this world, 'e lay on 'is hands and she rose, castin' off the plague like bed sheets."

Miracles - the easiest way to explain the inexplicable. They all wanted miracles. The dying, the sick, their loved ones, the well-wishers, the on-lookers, the rumour mongers, because a miracle was a story you could tell forever. Oh they wanted miracles, they wanted them so bad they built their own from scraps of marketplace gossip, the fumes of bar-room bravado, fragments weaved from collective needs.

"Tha say 'e appears outta thin air…'e wears a white robe that glows…'e can cure the pestilence with 'is spittle."

But with gratitude came suspicion, so easily wrought into fear. Since the rumours he ducked through the streets hooded and cloaked. Half the village sought his services and the other half his head. He didn't blame them, it was the nature of folk to bifurcate during crisis - some needed hope, others a scapegoat.

"Well ar 'eard 'e put a curse on the guards at tha bridge, snuck in to the village and is *spreadin'* the pestilence."

There was a line between saint and shyster being drawn in the sand, but it was as transient as a tidal mark.

As Father John drew himself up to the churchyard to meet Father Malone, shadows stretched across the cliffs. There was something wrong with the sky. The smothering grey, replaced by a fierce chiaroscuro. He tipped his hat to Edward who was hanging a black-brown seal pelt at the gate to disperse the clouds. Surely any trace of superstitious alchemy had now deserted the desiccated hide…and yet, and yet. Though there'd be no change in the weather there would be one in their mood. Wasn't it the same leavening of despair he was hoping to inspire?

'Oh I don't believe these simple minded tales" Father John had said, "but if the people think the Lord blessed you with the power to heal the sick then shouldn't you use that belief to generate some much needed good will?"

The Stranger demurred. He didn't want to re-enact some crowd pleasing charade. Father John had countered, not by citing the sanctuary he offered, the risks he was taking or even their long standing friendship, but with one well chosen question – 'then why *did* you come back?"

In his room above The Ship, Bull was equally dismissive of reputed resurrections.

'Ah cheap tricks! When I was in Scandinavia I saw a magician make a man float and a dog disappear' – and yet also pondering the power of suggestibility and the possibility of performing a little miracle of his own. "Spread the word' he told his men "that tomorrow at dawn I'll be outside the parish hall giving food to the needy."

Almost 800 people jostling for position, bellies were empty, tempers were fraught, and their cart was nearly overturned.

"Whadda we do" asked Fergus unnerved "we 'aven' gor enough te feed this lot?" Even Bull was taken aback, but the muskets under the tarpaulin were a great comfort.

"'Ow many loaves 'ave we got?...An 'ow many fishes? Ar want yus to walk among the crowd 'andin' out bread to everyone, an ar want ye to give a fish to..." he looked through the crowd choosing the recipients "...Eli Wallace... Malik Turner...Scapper...no, not Scapper, 'e'll be pissed. Give one te 'is missus, Kathy, she's gorra big family, an a big mouth. An give one to Geordie, tell 'im to share it with the auld fellas from the banjo pier...an one to..."

They said Bull's eyes were like coal, but at times they had a charismatic glint more like Whitby Jet.

"On second thoughts, leave the fishes, ar'll 'and 'em out meself."

Why, Crawshaw wondered, when only two days ago he was spooning out the eyes of a sheep and boiling its head to make soup, was Bull handing out fishes like the boat had just come in; but he didn't say anything, no one did, they just shoved closer to the cart and hoped to land a whopper. As Bull had suspected, in such straitened circumstances, hunger had silenced the conscience, and his strategic distribution had enlisted unwitting delegates in his bid to quiet insurgents. For those who shared Crawshaw's querulousness he was sending a slightly stronger message - *I* decide who deserves fish. Bull climbed up on the back of the cart, surveying his benevolence with a swell of pride and a beatific smile. He swept a forearm majestically across the scene and said "Gather up the leftovers boys!" Garside looked at his empty basket and gave Fergus a look from under his brow that said: "what fuckin leftovers!" but remained inaudible, reluctant to return to eating cattle feed. Fergus decided to humour Bull the best he could, for fear that the next thing he put in his mouth would be his dismembered penis.

The power of suggestion is a mysterious force, and as talk of Bull's generosity circulated, the quotidian bread made way for the more satisfying meat of the story until it became known as 'Bull and the Fishes'. Still the 'miracle' was secondary, the stunt fulfilled its primary purpose later that day when Lizzie Baker exchanged what she knew for one cod up front and one on his capture.

As Bull and his men marched up to St Hild's a crowd 20 strong had gathered by Market Street. Bull's rabble rousing also gathered momentum.

"We're doin' the town a service" he said. "He doesn't belong here, he's a foreign element, poisonous, killing this town – he's a canker that needs cutting out."

They'd been chasing the Stranger for over two weeks now, ever since he'd snuck through The Bridge, but every time they got a tip off he managed to evade them, always one step ahead. Bull was determined it wouldn't happen again. He'd had a man watching St Hild's for days, but no signs of coming and going.

"Breathing! That's what we came to witness!"

Greedy for miracles, Malone had mouthed all the right platitudes to access this exclusive gathering, but came prepared to be critical and knowing if his faith proved misplaced. Envy turned to cynicism, and as a Catholic Priest, he felt compelled to scorn the efforts of his Protestant counterpart, but he did so whilst avoiding this strange fellow's eyes.

Six of them, praying as the Stranger entered, and as he urged them up off their knees it was clear two would be lucky to see out the week. The best he could do was *escort* them to the other side.

"Show some respect Father" warned Father John, "No one promised anything here tonight. I just thought he might be able to help these people with what he learned on his travels." Malone may have been echoing his own reservations, but they were motivated by rivalry not concern. *He* shouldn't be so quick to judge because if the rumours were true, he'd been exchanging bottled holy water for food.

The Stranger showed them techniques he'd learnt from a Chinaman in Syria. Imagine your body is filling up with light...They sat straight backed in the pulpits with their eyes lightly closed, clearing their minds. Wondrous light that pours into your lungs and washes your soul with every breath...A Chinaman who'd taught him how to use the mind to generate warmth and positivity, to achieve serenity and eventually transcend the body and look down on the corporeal husk. Transcendence was rare and hard-earned, but at the least he knew the technique offered a communion with the self that left people feeling cleansed, empowered and eased their pain. He wasn't a doctor... it was all he could offer.

"I know several pilgrims who travelled to the Holy Land to treat the sick" Malone continued, "and none of them came back, and yet you would have us believe he worked amongst plague victims for years and returned unscathed".

All stillness broken, they blinked back into their darkened plight. The Stranger ended the meditation with a hand of apology and walked off down the aisle leaving the clergymen to argue. He ambled down through the Chancel Arch and into the North Chapel to gaze at the stained glass saints and pray for patience. Those days when he walked indestructible, untouchable through nightmare shielded like the canonized – where were they now? Malone was wrong to question the veracity of his pilgrimage, but he was right to question his power.

All exits covered. Bull came in by the South Porch, Fergus and Crow the West, Garside and Carter the Clergy Vestry. This time he'd planned, they weren't going to lose him again. Father John reached out for the pew, his body shaking visibly, and said a silent prayer. Would the Lord spare him this time? The next few moments were such a blur of almost visionary fear that he never noticed Malone give Bull a discreet nod towards the North Chapel. They had him in the cod-end.

Bull strode purposefully down the aisle but hesitated at the Chancel Arch, reluctant to violate the sanctuary of the church and confused by his reluctance. What was holding him back? His distrust of miracles seemed to have softened now that he'd 'done one', but he was increasingly seduced by the conviction that forces too powerful, too inexplicable to be earthly were at work here. What if this man was as good as they said, what if he could do *real* miracles.

"Come out peacefully" he called across the threshold: "There's no way out this time, we've got you surrounded" and it echoed around the nave.

They had to take him alive, it wouldn't reflect favourably, he suspected, to butcher a holy man in the House of God. He crossed himself and stepped in to finally confront his nemesis. Bull was disappointed but Father Malone got his 'miracle', because despite their searching every stone of the church, the Stranger had vanished.

Simony

A little white boat on a black sea. Sails hanging lifeless, it peeks around the banjo pier like an uninvited guest and spends the next 30 minutes creeping into the harbour. By the time it does a coble is rowing out to meet it. Bull astride the prow issuing directions to his crew, Garside, Carter and, shanghaied by blackmail and bribery onto Bull's implacable flagship – Father Malone.

Since the Stranger's escape Bull had stopped trying to buy Father John's services and was now puzzling how to kill the cleric without arousing suspicion in the villagers who'd heard his murderous threats that night…he'd know how when the time was right. Instead he directed his attentions to the other side, the other side of the Market Square were Malone ran St Mary's Church Roman Catholic Church.

Something unexpected happened to Malone that night when Bull and his men burst into St Hild's – torches blazing in the cold candlelight, a visceral flash shattering the forced serenity, the frightened piety – he was excited. He dismissed such silliness but felt a surge of empowerment later when Bull mentioned 'business propositions'. He couldn't refuse - literally. In Bull's presence, everything compressed. Malone's mind was freighted with pressure. His thoughts clouded – no…more of a shadow, a hefty shadow eclipsing his judgment.

The sea, mirroring the dark clouds, was transformed into a thick stout and the air dense with portent, an intense stillness, stifled calm. The town was petrified. The stasis crackled as the boatmen oared slowly towards the unknown, superstition dogging their every stroke. Malloy winced as Bull frowning trailed his fingers in the slurry, then gagged when he inexplicably cupped his hands and swilled his face and hair in the vile sludge.

Steadying himself against the hull, Bull shouted for the crew to show themselves. He indicated and Carter fired a shot into the air. Nothing. He gave Garside a nod to climb aboard and the henchman's face creased with conflicting fears. The ropes stretched, the deck creaked, the water lapped, lapped, lapped, lapped...and in that moment Bull realized several things

Why the boat looked familiar

Why their guns were useless

Why their fear needed relocating

Why he had absolutely nothing to fear.

In that suspension of time was the intimation of apocalypse but Bull vaulted aboard - he could see his trajectory, knew he'd clear the rim by the necessary millimeters - with cavalier flair.

He smelt it first then he saw it face down in the doorway. He turned the body over and, as he suspected, it stared him straight in the eye – death, as black as the brine.

He heard his name in a searching moan from down in the hold. Lying amid sacks of vegetables swigging a bottle of gin was Tully - one of three brothers Bull had been using to smuggle goods down from Buckhaven - his face too bore the increasingly familiar black boils death mask. His enquiry confirmed, he became agitated and frantic reaching out for help.

"Bull! Bull! Ach ar dinna believe it! Bull! Will ye tell me ma Bull! Can ya do that for me? Bull? Please Bull I beg ye – tell 'er for me. Tell 'er I'm sorry Bull, can ye? Tell 'er"

"Yeah, yeah, of course Tully, of course, relax. I'll tell 'er I promise. Calm down man, get a 'old o yerself – listen! What 'appened man, wha 'appened?"

"It got us, got us all, the whole toon. Me ma Bull, tell 'er ar never meant to 'urt 'er – not once. Ar couldna 'elp it ma, ar couldna 'elp it…"

Bull leant over his shoulder and shouted for assistance.

"Garside! Malone! Get in 'ere!"

Tully was still gabbling away, half-drunk, half mad with regret, as plague and dehydration fought to see who'd lay claim to his soul.

"This man needs 'elp Malone an it looks like yer the only one who can provide it now."

Stepping into the shadows and noticing the pestilence Malone hesitated and reconsidered his ecclesiastical duties under the weight of fear.

"Are ye a fuckin' man of God or a coward! Don't worry, ye don' 'av te fuckin' touch 'im, just give 'im the rights before 'e goes so he can die in peace…giv 'im a fuckin' blessin'!"

Malone reached inside his cassock, took out a bottle of holy water, splashed a cruciform across the stricken man and started with the Latin. Bull disgusted snatched the bottle from his hands, crouched, cradled Tully's head and lifted the water to his parched lips. Malone gaped at Henderson. *He'd* kept his distance from the sickness, even Father John had shown a sensible reluctance, and yet here was Bull embracing it!

"Go on now, yer saved. This man's a priest. Ye made yer peace wi' the Lord. Ye gonna be okay…Tell me wha 'appened?"

"Thank ye Father, thank you! God bless ye, God bless ye!"

"Tully! What 'appened?

"Crazy, dyin', rapin', killin'. We thought we were clever, careful…only went te town at night, to rob. The sickness got us. No escape. It's on the boat! Be careful Bull. Be careful!"

They checked the hold and found a considerable cargo of vegetables, grain and a few barrels of hooch – Bull's usual order.

"Garside, start unloadin' the stuff inte the boat."

Garside stood rigid, enraged, unable to speak, all his energies redeployed in resisting Bull's will. He shot a determined look that, for the split second before he was forced to lower it, communicated to Bull that he still had a splinter of backbone.

Malone voiced Garside's mute disapproval: "We can't sell this!" Bull glared at him and he delivered the remainder of his reservations towards the deck.

"You can't feed them that - it's poisonous! It's infected with pestilence!"

"Aye and mor'n likely cursed an all!" shouted Carter from the coble.

Fortified Garside finally managed to blurt out his opposition "It's murder! You berra kill me now 'cos ar'll 'ave no part of it!"

If he'd needed to explain why he never punished their mutiny summarily then their muskets would have sufficed, but in truth his brain was already busy redrafting his tactics.

"Supply and demand – that's wha' life's all about. When the people are in need then someone 'as te satisfy that need. This time that someone's me."

He placed a hand on their shoulders and guided them gently back to the coble. He chuckled, amused to see they weren't entirely spatchcocked.

"They need law n order – they come to me. They need food or drink – they come to me, they need 'ope...well..."

When they'd safely disembarked he grabbed Morgan's hooch and splashed it around the boat.

"They need 'ope – they turn te God...but 'e doesn' seem to be listenin, does 'e *'oly man?*"

"Why are you doing all this" said Malone "you must have all the money?"

"Aye, but I don' 'ave all the power," he stopped, shot a terrifying glare at Malone and said coldly "you...are gonna 'elp me get it."

Finished with the hooch he took the torch from Carter's hand and said: "Those people are dyin', they 'ave no use fe money, food, goods – why deny them 'appiness before they go?"

He threw the torch into the hold and watched calmly as it exploded out onto deck. "The bones of a saint can be kissed for an 'apenny and bought for tuppence." They could hear Tully's screams.

"I'll get the bones, you do the rest." And he waited, waited…waited - until his colleagues squirmed with anxiety – laughing amid the flames.

Tide was Turning

The soil was dead. The sea was dry. The fruit was withering on the vine. The light was fading and hope. Two children had found a burlap sack full of human hair and teeth. The parents came with questions in their eyes and all he could do was compound them.

"What does it all *mean* Father? What's the Lord trying to tell us?"

He stood on The Bluffs and stared out to sea. What *does* it all mean? What do we *really* know? What can we claim as true? That the sun will rise each day? The sun was long gone. That the seasons will change? They'd vanished too. That God will provide...?

Their little boy wouldn't move, wouldn't talk, sat, there but elsewhere, spittle on his chin. Like the beasts, the fish and the daylight he'd withdrawn.

Witchcraft? There were the usual whispers. God? Was the Lord angry with them? The Devil? They could sense him in the streets.

They needed reassurance. It was his job to find order in chaos. The Nicene Creed. Filioque. 'From the Father through the Son'. Christ died for our sins according to the Scriptures, and He was buried and raised on the third day...according to the Scriptures. Why then were they still being punished?

Original sin? Too original for Father John, cornered by religious certainties, ill-equipped to deal with the unpredictable. He was foundering - alone, abandoned, out of his depth. Disquiet had festered for weeks, but today doubt solidified into crisis. What was the Lord trying to tell him, them? Clues, inscrutable clues, seemed commonplace, but not heaven sent. Armageddon, apocalypse, rapture - *something* was nigh and all he could see at the end of the tunnel was darkness.

Down on the rocks, Rarfie was suffering no such compunctions. He'd had an idea, and set off for the Black Sands with his bucket and spade.

"Where the 'ell ye goin Rarfie?" Cooper cried as they passed on Middlegate. "What's the point of diggin for bait when ye know there's nowt te catch?"

Rarfie smiled and walked on, he had his plan, a plan that would feed his family - if cod could eat it then so could they.

"Go on ye fuckin' la la!" shouted Cooper over his shoulder by way of good-bye.

'My father died when I was eight. He'd always been a very religious man, whereas I, well, though I never dared voice my opinions… I was - unconvinced. He was, well, he would have loved to have been a priest, but back in his day that was…impossible."

Joe and Maggie needed direction. They'd become a daily presence in the church, lighting candles, reciting prayers, fasting, but to no avail. What could he say? Their existence was wrapped around that child?

One minute he was dumbfounded, the next he was sharing his darkest hour: "The day they buried him I was standing outside the church and the sun-light was coming through the trees and felt this tremendous release, a weight gradually lifting from my shoulders. I had this overwhelming sense that father was with the Lord, and yet also, with me, and always would be. I felt waves of love washing over my body and…and *knew*, for a *fact*, that things *happen* for a *reason*'.

His father's death - his nadir and his apogee. Every time he lit a candle he thanked his da' for showing him the way. He'd felt reborn. Since then he'd walked in the ways of his father, not turning to the left or to the right.

"It wer' bloody decent of God to fix it for you" Joe spat, "but d'ye not think 'e might get off 'is arse now an 'elp the rest o' us."

He was right. These were caliginous times - was he trying to relight their faith or rekindle his own? He felt so impotent - their son was stuck – what could he do? He'd reconsecrated the church, removing and purifying anything considered unclean. They'd given their first fruits of grain, new wine, oil, honey, all that the fields produced. They'd burnt offerings morning and night, yielding crops to the flames when the livestock were gone, gifts when the food grew scare, and he'd felt guilty (while Bull gave out bread) for sapping their resources. They'd sung His praises in the holy dwelling place till their throats were sore and yet none of their prayers reached Heaven.

'E's got some misguided priorities 'as this Lord of yours Father."

And that was it – he was losing them. Just like their son they were distancing themselves from divinity. No matter how many he'd coaxed into mass, they didn't want enlightenment, theirs wasn't the pursuit of truth, of meaning, they just wanted things to go back to normal.

He'd come full circle and found himself back on The Bluffs. By the rocks Rarfie had laid down his shovel and was ranting and gesticulating wildly at the sea, his crude oaths lost in the wind. Wearily he slumped down onto a rock and started winnowing through kelp and shells. Descending to the beach, Father John thought he might ease the pain of at least one troubled soul. As he lay his hand on Rarfie's shoulder he glanced up, briefly registered his presence and put some moss in his mouth. The clergyman sat down beside him and stared forlornly out to sea.

Rarfie sneezed into his hands, then drawing them back like a prayer book to reveal a votive offering of green and red, he very deliberately lent forward and licked it up. Shaking with weakness, Father John reached into his pocket for a handful of corn and offered half to Rarfie.

"Even the ragworms Father…even the ragworms." They'd become used to enduring Rarfie's ramblings with good grace, but head shaking and tearful, he seemed uncharacteristically distraught.

"…and the sea's not coming back either."

What was he…? Father John realised how long he'd been walking The Bluffs - it must have been a while…including the time at his father's grave… a *long* while. The gloom had closed in, but the tide hadn't moved a foot.

The slack water just stood there, stagnant, challenging him to make his move. A sign, a message, a test? Deuteronomy 10:20. The saviour in the desert. 'All these things I will give you if you fall down and do an act of worship to me.'

Not again? He listened for the Lord's voice in his head, but he was no Moses and no Canute neither. There were forces beyond knowing operating in this town, forces to which even Mother Nature must bow.

The tide *was* turning, but no more, because it had turned. Everything had turned – away, upside down, inside out, back to front. Black was white, day was night, good was bad and wrong was right. The Darkness needed feeding and they must pay their tithe.

The Unburied

She checked Ethan before she went to bed, still feverish, and sealed the door with seaweed. Scurrying back from the well next morning she turned to see a big white cross daubed on her wall and dropped the bucket in fright. More of an X than a cross she thought as she shakily refilled, but the message was unmistakable: they'd been marked, and they needed help before nightfall or a slow death from plague would be a blessing they'd never count.

But where could she turn, all their friends were dead or disappeared. They backed into their homes, barricaded the windows and wrapped themselves in prayer, but it was too late, they were already shrouded in pestilence.

Cracks appeared.

Their land, their very roots, had been shaken; allegiances like tectonic plates shifted; fault lines divided the town into factions. Long forgotten boundaries reasserted, deeply etched animosities tore across the map. Fissures zigzagged down Church Street and along Hild and Brus splitting the Croft, the Lanes and the Gate into shards. The trickle of Three Mills Stream became a Rubicon between the north and south and the cottages beyond the woods seemed insurmountable.

Fights for food grew from squabbles and scuffles to stabbings and beatings and kinsmen foraged in packs. Festering rivalries erupted, sparking a conflagration of killings that rampaged unchecked until Bull imposed a curfew. When the gloaming pitched the streets emptied.

Ethan had been with his brother Dan scouring the threshing fields for wheat. He returned with three ears of corn and some handfuls of bran which he mashed up into porridge. He forced most onto her and then, still weak with hunger, went off to search the rubbish behind the Quay sheds. He staggered back an hour later shivering and retching.

His temperature shot up that night but fell on the second day and stablised the third. There were no lumps in the groin or armpits and Cass was relieved – he'd eaten a rancid fish head - it was poison not plague, but the cross showed someone demurred. Someone in the neighbourhood, some self appointed physic had misdiagnosed them as dirty and tonight they would be 'cleansed'.

She stared at the unmatched brickwork were Ethan and Dan repaired the kitchen wall from the ruins of Shepton Rectory. She didn't trust his wife, not since her third daughter was born with teeth, but she felt she could rely on Dan. They'd only made it this far thanks to the provisions he'd sensibly stockpiled before the animals fled. What she would give now for just one of those eggs they'd eaten two at a time before they understood the difference between hunger and starvation.

Soon she wasn't looking at anything and she wasn't thinking of anything. Time passed though no one could say how much, then she stood up, adjusted her self like a chair or an undergarment, took a carving knife from the drawer and set off.

1&2: Limbo and Lust

The green fields were gone. The once verdant pastures deracinated by the famished, demented with malnutrition, dazed and docile, gravitating towards the meadows grazing. Minds had been lost, evicted by grief and empty shells bereft of hope or understanding wandered like untethered sheep.

She waded through a patch of long grass. In the clearings the hungry picked carefully through old cow dungs for kernels of corn; the hungrier, not so carefully.

She startled to find a woman squatting with her skirts round her waist shitting diarrohea with a mouthful of weeds. Fascinated and fearful she studied the bovine expression untroubled by shame.

Any herbs were gone, along with the choicest grass. Foliage too had been stripped from the trees, until the woods had become a dumping ground for the dead. Now malodour repelled some, malevolence the others. The Beast shifted amongst the trees.

He wasn't gonna die a virgin. Why should he? He'd waited. He'd stayed away from the whores like his da said and now he was being punished for his patience? It wasn't fair. Everyone was doing it. Fuck the gangs! Fuck the curfew! If he was going to die then he had to do this one thing first, he had to die a man.

He'd snook down to the Quay twice, skulking in the shadows, but the whores were long gone and there were no women scavenging. She was gonna die anyway - they all were – then what did it matter? He waited in the Yew bushes, watching her approach, with his cock in his hand.

She struggled with her dress folds, clumsily freed her knife and clutched it two-handed, awaiting an attack...that never came. The frenzy, all hers, was tempered by his strange stillness. She lowered her knife and he stepped forward with a half turn, allowing light into his cowl. What was wrong with his face? No plague? No hunger?...he was smiling!

He held out his hand and she almost passed him the knife until he said, to her, to himself, to posterity: "Midway on life's journey, I found myself in dark woods, the right road lost". She sought guidance and this, she decided, was it. She took his hand, and as he led her in, the branches seemed to part revealing an unforeseen path. Fear crept up her spine a bone at a time, then, hanging from a tree, something more carrion than man found a quicker route. She crouched, clutching his robe, and waves of steaming vomit splashed up onto her shins. She wiped bile from her chin with the back of her hand and would've laid down and died if not for Ethan. That seaweed wouldn't last him long.

3. Gluttony

You eat it or die. You eat it or die. It's only meat. Eat it or die. Just the flesh of a dead animal. The unwanted flesh of a dead animal. There was no face now. Just the flesh of a dead animal. A dead animal. He thought it would be easier. He'd found the body lying there. He hadn't even killed him.

4. Greed

Bull knew there was a rumour that the woods were infested with demons, because he'd started it. He'd seen it - before the animals fled, before the land died - he'd known how it would all end. He'd always known. 'You can take their money away,' he'd told his men cryptically, 'but you can't take it with you – it's no good there.' It was on his nod Stubbs traded liquor for chickens and Malone's collection plate coffers became swollen with foodstuffs. And, of course, the Scottish imports continued until they stopped.

But where to hoard it – boxes of vegetables had already spoiled in the dank of Stubbs' cellar? There was a disused mill in the woods, where they'd tortured and killed their victims, the stifled screams replaced now with corn and potatoes.

At first Bull thought it prudent to conceal his…methods, so Malone's congregation began to see things through the trees, suggested things - by Bull, then Malone - began to manifest themselves in the minds of the pious, until, by collective public opinion, the Stranger was convicted of black magic; but since it had become impossible to divide the pestilent from the murdered, since the façade of humanity had slipped, Bull no longer needed to demonise others, he was more concerned with the demons on *his* back.

Stubbs' daughter was starving. Garside's sister was starving. Everyone was starving yet hoards of fruit were rotting in the barn. What was holding them back? Stubbs knew, he wasn't ashamed to say…fear. The overweight publican would sweat and shake when Bull was in the room and he'd wept involuntarily – two single tears rolled down his cheeks - after the last time they'd talked.

His cellar was bare. Stubbs knew of the barn but he dare not touch it. Bull usually kept him well stocked, but he hadn't been seen for two days. Stubbs would rather have laid there and starved than ever face Bull again, but he couldn't watch his daughter do it. He contacted Bull's cronies, Garside and Crow, two of the few men in the village with the strength left to resist.

5. Anger

With the rags round their faces they looked like outlaws, but they also served a practical purpose – doused in piss to ward off the putrescence. They shot one guard in the belly, and as they watched him die the other realigned. They were gorging themselves on rotten apples when Bull arrived - alone, unarmed, strolling about the clearing singing a nursery rhyme off key. They barred the door and readied their muskets at the window.

"Yer already dead" Bull shouted "and yer know it – yer just not buried yet…maybe ye never will be, and we know wha 'appens to them poor basteds. Stubbs, throw down ye gun and ar'll see that ye lie in St Mary's next to yer father and grandfathers. Isn't that what ye've always wanted, te live up te yer ancestors? Cowards and swindlers every one.

"Crow, I know you, I know 'ow ye mind works, ye're already wonderin whether te run for it. Run, ye know wha ar'll do when ar catch yer. Come out now and ar'll kill ye quick, none of the unpleasantness.

"Garside, *you're* mine, and ar'll see ye in 'ell soon enough, but who else shall ar bring along wi me – ye whore, Kelly…ye sister Clare… ye granddaughter Emma."

A shot flew by, then shouting and struggling in the barn. There was none of the manic laughter from Bull – herding sinners was serious business – but as he toyed with their lives there was the thinnest sardonic smile.

6. Heresy

He imagined the queues outside heaven…or the other place. The climate had changed – physically and metaphysically - they were all wading through sin. The soul dies with the body. The heretics would be 'trapped in flaming tombs', but looking around at the corpses Father John almost hoped they were right.

If God had willed it this way then it was foolish to resist. He just had to do this one thing, to restore the balance. He had to make this sacrifice. It was the Christian thing to do. He had a date to keep, a date that they'd failed to keep so many times, but this time he knew it was waiting – Judgment Day.

7. Violence

"C'mon boy, come an get me!" Bull stood out in the clearing with his arms aloft inviting death. "Now's ye chance! I'm gonner slice that child up like a kipper!"

There was more shouting and fighting, another shot rang out, then silence.

"Garside, ye remember when we buried yer auld man? When ar took care of it for ye? That was tough man. Ar knew 'im since ar was a boy. Ardest thing I ever ad to do…so ar didn't bother."

For the first time they noticed that Bull had a sack with him. He bent down, untied the rope and unfurled the hessian to reveal a partially decomposed corpse.

Garside flew out the mill in a rage but Bull side stepped and casually kicked him under the kneecap. As he stumbled, Bull swung round and hit him across the back of the head with a shovel, killing him with one blow. He sauntered up to the barn oblivious to the shots that whistled past his ears. They frantically tried to reload, ramrodding the barrel, gunpowder peppering the floor, but when Bull appeared they stood, heads bowed, guns by their side, waiting to die.

Crow started to cry. Bull put a paternal arm around his shoulder, tousled his curly hair and dislocated his spinal column from his brain. He turned his gaze onto Stubbs who, shaking and sweating, fumbled almost dropped the bayonet before stabbing himself in the stomach, slumping to his knees with a smile. He didn't care where his soul went as long as it wasn't there.

He looked down on Stubbs' body – so peaceful – with a mix of omnipotence and envy. In death a man who'd lived as a coward had finally taken control of his own destiny, or had he? It was all getting too easy. Three more corpses – but no matter how many people he killed or tortured, it didn't help, he wouldn't be satisfied until they were all dead, including him.

8. Fraud

Joseph was crying, writhing and gnashing in confession. He'd found and ear of corn and ate it alone crouched in the woods while his wife and daughter starved at home. As he twisted to untangle his conscience from the guilt, Malone envied the simplicity of his predicament.

Twice daily the devout smeared themselves with ashes and wriggled on their bellies along Hart Road. He sold them holy relics - bones from 'saints'; Easter candle amulets to ward off infection; dispensing absolution and blessings, though they had nothing left to give.

He'd promising to bury the dead, those without living relatives had come to him terrified that their souls would wander in limbo. Their final wish to be laid to rest and he was violating their last rites.

They followed the trail of dead through the gloom: An old man, limbs splayed at unnatural angles; a familiar young woman face down who she dare not turn; a child. The unburied scattered through the woods like breadcrumbs.

She stumbled in ashen, and though Dan questioned her she was unable to speak, only shake her head. She felt fatigued, weary, tired of fighting. She'd seen things in the woods that shouldn't be seen. She just wanted to go to sleep. She just wanted to go to Heaven.

The Ninth Circle (Treachery)

If it's not one thing, then it's another.

He'd always eschewed his mother's Manichean homily, but it had all come down to this - he had to make a choice, he had to make a sacrifice - because the truth was they'd paid much more than a tithe and they'd continue to pay until someone brought it to an end.

They were slitting their own throats, they were hanging from the trees, they were stood on the sand with stones in their pockets - he had to do it to save the village. Besides, he was only setting the scene, introducing the elements, precipitating the inevitable - the rest was in…God's hands.

On a burnt out sphere, in the middle of the wood, at the edge of the world they stood. Stasis hardened, static cracked, and they prowled the peripheries like estrus cats. Diametrical forces turning in opposition. The push and the pull, the pro and the contra, the twist of dark and light trapped in an eternal cycle.

Dizzy he crouched to pray, and considered the Old Testament sinners who bowed to false gods. Good and evil - the axis on which the world spun, constantly, confusingly, revolving. Had he been genuflecting in the wrong direction?

Where was the power and great glory that the Gospels spoke of? He will rescue us from the coming wrath, from the lawless one and then he will reward each person according to what he has done. Where was the rescue? How long must they wait? The gifts were given according to God's sovereign will, and it was clear who was holding all the charism? Regal, magisterial - princeps tenebrarum. If this was the reckoning, then how would it tally? Maybe, he hoped, now he'd humbled himself for the common good, there might be a little something left for him.

Father John watched from the fringes of history, flanked by ghosts, haunted by conscience. An intense humming droned in his head like a horde of flies. Flickering phantasms so real he tried to swat them away. Whispers? - his father heard the voice of God, guiding - he strained to hear their bidding. But in this forsaken place could he even be sure it was the Lord, because no matter how often he looked over his shoulders he saw neither devil nor angel.

With the ceremonial steps of a medieval dance they converged. Advance and retreat, echo and counter, traversing an invisible labyrinth, coiled like a clock mechanism counting down. Almost full circle, they met in the middle. Fish in a bucket, twins in a womb, curled almost touching in a courtly courtship.

Another voice at his shoulder and in a moment unnoticed they snap to a clinch, spiral, wrestling, teetering, and yet finding an unlikely balance in the twist of symbiosis. As they reeled around, back and forth, his senses lurched and scended, reality upended. Soaring? Falling? He checked the ground, it was still there.

Storm whipped dust and the grey sky spun into a vortex of ash. As the darkness laminated, he lost the melee in the density. A bolt of lightning cracked down through the clouds like the reaper's boney finger and a shock of illumination struck the dead land. The earth shuddered, groaned and steamed like a cooling corpse. Sprites danced, halos fanned, and as a duality of wave and particle flashed through the trees, perception slowed to a montage of broken images. He felt a shift inside. He'd been so busy anticipating a rearguard attack he hadn't expected the enemy within. And the whispers - "what you do, do quickly."

He pushed the heels of his hands into his eyes. Concentric silver coils pulsed behind the lids, and as he blinked half blind through the tears and confusion he swore he saw Bull lean in and kiss the Stranger.

Sinews stretch, muscles meld, limbs twist, tear, split. Contorted, distorted, contrary forces merged into a snarling singular beast. The thrash of wings, the scream of angels, and for one petrified frame he blenched to see his own bloodless face atop the chimera - an unholy alliance of lion, scapegoat and serpent.

Was this his vision – *now?* He couldn't believe it. *Now!*

He looked to the heavens for hope - lightning flashed from the east to the west - and then unfurling from the horizon like a rolling scroll across the fundamental constant of nature, until - atere, atere - he tumbled into the abyss.

Sheep on his right, goats on his left. The righteous and the wicked. Damnation, jubilation the gathered nations, separation.

Vivid images, swam in an out, up an down as he drifted in the slack water.

Seven angels, seven plagues…a sea of glass mixed with fire…the wrath of God, who lives forever.

He was ready. Ready for the judgment. Ready to be punished, to be cleansed of sin. Ready for the end, ready to begin. He was ready for eternity or, so be it, purgatory.

Sever the silver cord, break the golden bowl, shatter the spring pitcher, break the wheel at the well, and the dust returns to the ground, and the spirit to He who gave it…

A distant point of luminosity demanded linearity. He relaxed, released, washing away *carrying the soul to Abraham's Bosom,* but an overwhelming undertow just wouldn't let him go, and *a beast with ten horns stood on the shore…*

In Genesis, God divided the light from the darkness…but the real and the unreal were inseparable.

He staggered around the rim of consciousness. His head spun. His senses betrayed him. He exchanged absolute darkness for an intense absence of light. He stood paralysed, incapable of choice. No matter how many times he blinked all he could see behind his eyelids was the repeated image of him cowering beneath a barrage of stones and persecution. *They* knew nothing of faith, its complications. It was all Heaven and Hell to them.

With a double edged sword to his throat, Bull forced the Stranger down to the sea. Crouched in the bracken Father John watched him spit a mouthful of blood and a gobbet of flesh rolled, coating in dust. Strange but he swore he could taste the Eucharist wine.

Those whispers again, but what were they saying…justice - or Judas?

Deus ex Machina

In the beginning was the word, and by the end a sentence - a death sentence. The village wanted him dead. They'd made their feelings know, lodged their petitions. They'd asked, and they had received. After 40 days of inexplicable evasion, he had been delivered.

Scorched, black cinder, crunched underfoot; plumes of smoke and brimstone thickened overhead; copper methane stench as blood boiled in fetid corpses; darkness expanded across a charred wasteland, scattered funeral pyres shed no light, and they were lost, consumed, impastoed against the sepulchral backdrop like shadows in the night.

They emerged from the cracks, scurrying like rats, following Bull down to the sea. Distraction from the clamour, sobbing, screaming, carnage. Outside St Hild's they bound his hands behind his back, clasped him tight around the neck and marched him to the shore. Brutal forearms struggled so hard to contain this elusive spirit that no one noticed his lack of resistance. Steaming women hissed and spat, scratched and kicked. Men jostled to land a punch and as they bundled him down the Southgate steps howling curses he lost his footing, head bouncing up off the limestone. Everything went black, and, as he arose awash with blood and nausea, stayed black: black and bleak and hopeless and black.

The darkness enveloped them, folding and enfolding. A region of space and time distorted, twisting their humanity into unrecognizable shapes, compressing them into a corner where it crept up through the souls of the feet, devouring inside, until all that remained was absence operating in a void. A region of space and time distorted, sucking them towards a conclusion until not even light could escape, not even the final ray of hope. A bottomless pit black where once was chiaroscuro.

Nothing is true, everything is permitted, the assassins silently screamed as they kicked and thrashed him down to the coal black sea. He fell to his knees, the lacerating sting of a knotted rope across his back. They were out of control, but was anyone ever *in* control. The natural laws had been losing their influence for some time, and the Crofters losing their minds. Sacrificing a man to save themselves, seemed rational in the circumstances. If physics refused to comply, then why should conscience?

They barreled him into the sea, and when he came up spitting foam, reeling with concussion, he saw Bull on the shore with an oar and a noose like a perverted Justice. No words passed between his captors but they were unhindered by silence, going through the motions with an unspoken understanding. Dig the hole, plant the oar, sling the rope, test the noose – seamless, as though pre-planned, suffused with a sense of déjà vu.

Chilling screams in the distance, but all Father John could hear was the whisper of doubt, a fading echo of the holy. He'd lost his faith, and who was he without it? A personal narrative tightly bound up with the Lord was unravelling. Scripture spun around his head like yarn, but there were no words of salvation left. The Parables, the Psalms, Revelation – lost among the bloodlust. They were beyond communication, all instinct and now. *He'd* been recast as a quack at a dumb show, a charlatan at a mummery with no prompt. Wherefore art thou Lord? For 54 years he'd followed the word of God to the letter of the law, conducted a one-sided conversation with the almighty, providing his own guidance in lieu of replies. All his life he'd felt he was being ignored, but this was worse - he felt he wasn't.

It lay in His hands, but Father John – as always, pleading for the sign that would please his dad – had tried to force the hand of God and succeeded only in touching the defiling pitch of Ecclesiastes. But still he thought - if Kendall did see you laying out burnt animal bones in the woods, or Jenny Lambert and her daughter truly saw you throw a black cat from the belfry, then for God's sake perform some miracle now! He stood before them crossing himself frantically and as he threw himself to the ground he thought of the Sanhedrin and the trial. He clenched, kneeling in the fetal position like a fist, praying harder than ever.

Bull was inspired.

The one thing that stood between him and omnipotence would soon cease to exist. He had control, how could he fail? Everything was falling into place. The planets were aligning and he was orchestrating events, manipulating circumstance, tamping on happenstance, shaping destiny.

He could have torched him right there without a doubt, because that's what the Lord needed - men of action, born leaders unafraid to do His bidding, unafraid to cleanse, start afresh, stride with the single-minded vision into a new world, men who could kill without feeling, without guilt, without judgment. But something – an understanding, a realisation, an epiphany - jolted him from his resolution and made him wonder - what would they say, when this was all over, how would *he* be judged?

His ruthless reputation was secure, but that, he knew, wouldn't be enough this time. They feared him, but he wanted their respect, he needed their adulation. He stood on the cusp of eternity, and if he was to emerge with mythic status, he couldn't share the aftermath with a martyr.

His grip on the town had tightened to a stranglehold, he was the puppet master to the dancing marionettes, he was the maniacal cry that drown out the collective conscience, he was the power mad pervert stood amidst the flames of self-immolation fiddling…and, he was the benevolent sage handing choice to the people.

His psyche shifted. He considered his options. Which was true? Which was permitted? They all were, depending on what the future held. He felt like a God, but sometimes you had to leave judgment to the Lord…and sometimes it paid to make it seem as though you were.

Leading the stranger up the beach, Bull slowed, eyed the crowd, smiled and nodded to his men who dragged crab pots from a nearby coble and pushed the Stranger atop. Bull, serene, silent, majestic, tightened the noose around the palus, crossed himself and, with elaborate pantomime, washed his hands in the sea. It was with God now, a sign was sure to be given…and when it was Bull would be the first to see it.

In the darkest hour Father John's prayers had been answered - a hush had fallen. He looked up from his supplication. At the point of no return the baying mob had bridled and stood transformed, heads bowed, hands folded in their laps.

Nothing happened, then happened some more, and again. Stasis hardened, static cracked, A numinous tableau, frozen for posterity like insects in amber – like flies in jet.

He rejoined them in prayer, and, as he waited he rewrote his narrative to accommodate the miraculous. He hadn't lost his faith, he could see that now, clearly, from the other side, from this perspective, he'd experienced the most rigorous test of his life, and had emerged reborn.

Twice upon a time?

He'd been double crossed. He'd thought it might have been different now.

During the Exodus of Calcutta, as 80,000 women and children fled across the Sinai Desert to escape the Armenian army he'd locked the city gates behind them; when the earth shook and the City of Carthage crumbled he led the blind and crippled out to the river; he'd seen the attack ship fleets off the coast of Galicia before it was devastated; he'd seen the Bedouin fires at night, broken bread with the Ayatollah during the peace accord with the Macovites. So long ago now the events themselves had faded, only the stories remained - and *this* is how it was to end, because here his reputation was nothing. *A prophet is not without honor save in his own country*. The moment he stepped under the Bridge he'd felt enervated. He'd returned, with his wisdom, and they'd failed to appreciate him again.

Was he a prophet? They called him one, but if so, he was short-sighted seer. He'd watched it coming like a rider on the desert horizon but hadn't noticed the hood and scythe until too late. This was the end game, the Rapture, the final chapter. He must die – that much was clear. But who was responsible?

If this was a trial then who done it? They had a victim, they had a crime, they had a motive, but who was the killer? Whose hand signed his death warrant?

Was it sacrifice, murder or suicide?

Someone slashed his gown and tore it off, leaving a three inch gash across his side. Fear, like a hand, reached up inside him and his bowels spat shit all down his legs.

He'd had his chance. The day before last. The gate, unmanned in the entropy - he could have ran. He stood transfixed for...how long? A clear path right out of the village. He was free – he was going to do it – run. Yes, he would run and then settle down, live a normal life, free from the crushing gravitas of destiny. He could, he could run, he would, he would...he...he couldn't leave this town, he had a job to do. He was free, wasn't he? He would be soon. Free from a life sentence of piety, righteousness, isolation, infamy, an unbearable sense of immanence.

He cast around for the metaphor, the pattern that indicated what would happen next. When you'd lived a life that shone with significance – there was no such thing as coincidence, nothing was just what it was. The priest was right, everything *did* happen for a reason, but it was not always possible to figure out what that reason was. He felt a guiding hand so capricious it might just as well have been random.

He'd emerged victorious so many times he'd gotten used to it...but how could he ever forget what happened before. Paranoia was another pattern that lay just beneath the surface, always waiting for a chance to impose itself.

He'd seen blasphemers stoned to death, town's razed as burnt offerings, cities of women and children slaughtered – all in the name of the Lord, and struggled to understand the balance between good and evil.

Every gathering he walked into, heads turned, and he'd known from the beginning, known it was inevitable, the same way he'd known they were waiting for him, the villagers gathered impassively amongst the headstones as they passed the churchyard, like a Sunday service except with torches and pitchforks. There was a plot. Everyone was in on it, the universe wanted him dead and even God did nothing to prevent it. Everything had been building towards this, every event steered him towards this critical moment but he was powerless. All he wanted was a sign, a sign that his life hadn't been wasted.

Someone wiped blood from his eyes, he blinked them clean and for the first time he noticed they stood in a semi circle, heads bowed. What were they waiting for? Prayer! But he was too proud, refused to yield. This time he'd sworn he'd go it alone, like all self-respecting sons he refused to be over reliant on his father. If love was what it was really about, then He would make the first move.

Twenty three people on the beach that day lived to tell the tale and from that centrifugal source 36 different narratives shot out at the speed of sound splitting into scions as they went. Sub-dividing to audience needs, modulating mid story, twisting with memory, exaggerating in anecdote, fragmenting in doubt, conflating with other tales, crystallizing into surety, going mouth to mouth, offering resuscitation in recitation.

By midnight the next day those stories had multiplied to more than 1000. Who was responsible? – everyone. Reality shattered into myriad shards of experience, history was being repeatedly rewritten, as the end disappeared the beginning unfurled like the snake eating its ouroboric tale. Had he given them what they wanted? Ask and you shall receive? It wasn't that simple. Serious artists didn't work like that, didn't do requests. It was more improvised, democratic.

So this was how it had to be. In the beginning was the word, and by the end a sentence - a death sentence, a footnote in the annals of mythology.

Though he vowed not to voice it, in his delirium the song circled in his head - *"Eli Eli lama sabachthani?"* – My God, my God, why have you forsaken me? One word was all it would take, but as ever, the Lord it seemed, was speechless.

The End and Other Short Stories

"Listen now…"

The Elders were telling their stories again. Crouched round campfires or huddled at the hearth, always the same one: The Greatest Story Ever Told.

"…and the earth shook, and the sun turned black and the moon was like blood. And the people cried out and threw themselves to the ground and begged the Lord for mercy, for they truly thought their time had come."

They'd heard it all before. Every sitting unfolded the same way. Jethro or Amos or John would settle on a weather beaten sleeper and kindle up a tale from driftwood and sea coal. The day done, the fishermen dragged the boats up the sands to join them and as dusk neared the smaller boys gravitated towards the heat.

The Story to End All Stories they called it, but it didn't, because if you arrived too early you'd sit through endless rememberings; and if the beer came out they could go on until dawn.

It had been a long winter, Alfie hadn't heard it told since late last summer, so when he noticed it was Auld Jethro he haunched on the edge of the circle.

"They say the clouds parted on the horizon and a single beam of light shone down on them from on high…"

"E's doin it agen" whispered Tom.

"Doin wha?"

"Tellin it wrong."

"It's not wrong, it's jus…different."

"Well that's not ow John told it last year…or 'ow 'e told it last time either."

"Shhh" said Alfie, "I like this part."

Jethro elaborated, embroidered, but his furbelows were not to everyone's tastes. Twisting and turning without caution his tales were almost as gnarled as him. His fanciful style teetered, and toppled, into self-indulgent ramblings on everything from ill-fated fishing trips to how he got his scars and the 'many, many' women he had known.

"…they say he was seen a few days later walking out by the Bluffs in a white robe looking lost but very much alive."

Will was trying to listen but couldn't take his eyes off Jethro's mouth - the gap on the bottom row where his teeth should have been and the spittle in the corners of his mouth; so white, so unnaturally white. He drew circles in the sand with a stick and wished he'd gone home with his ma and sister.

Tom was about to leave to, but something held him back. For years Jethro had gotten away with it because he was an elder. It wasn't done to question. That was gonna end tonight.

"And the sky cleared and the sea calmed and a seagull came gliding back into the harbour carrying a leaf in its mouth…though some say it was a fish bone."

"…and is that a true story?"

The confident voice was a shock, even to Tom. His heart pounded, his mind spun. All the boys and most of the men were looking at him. Dizzy but defiant he stared into the flames until the fear passed. There was a hush and then every-one looked at Jethro to see what happened next. He shifted arse cheeks, prised open another mussel and continued in his usual style.

'Well son, no one knows for sure, but it wer told to me by my granddad Robert…and he never told me a lie. Now maybe if you had a strong enough telescope and a very sharp knife…but not I. When I was a boy I took a pocket watch apart, and it never worked again.'

He had more questions, but Jethro stood up, brushed sand from his lap and gathered his mussels in the sheet.

'Looks like rain. Let's go inside ey'. They stamped out the fire and made their way into the boathouse. Alfie helped them drag the nets. He looked around for Tom who was still standing by the fire explaining something to three other boys. He opened his mouth to call him but then declined. Something had changed. Maybe he wouldn't be around Tom so much anymore.

The Elders offered resurrection but the boys wanted post-mortem. Life goes on. It's not the end. It never is.

ISBN 978-1-907989-07-0

Lightning Source UK Ltd.
Milton Keynes UK
UKOW04f0640300914

239381UK00001B/20/P